The Mycroft Memoranda

The Mycroft Memoranda

A NOVEL BY
Ray Walsh

St. Martin's Press
New York

Library of Congress Cataloging in Publication Data

Walsh, Ray, 1949–
   The mycroft memoranda.

   I. Title.
PR9144.9.W34M9   1984   813'.54   84-18386
ISBN 0-312-55864-3

First published in Great Britain by André Deutsch Limited.

First U.S. Edition

10 9 8 7 6 5 4 3 2 1

to Sally with love

'What you do in this world is a matter of no consequence. The question is, what can you make people believe you have done?'

Sherlock Holmes (*A Study in Scarlet*)

CONTENTS

ACKNOWLEDGEMENTS

I wish to express my heartfelt thanks to my wife, Sally, for the help and support she has given me during the writing of this book. She has been, in turn, researcher, detective, critic, editor and copy-typist which in itself is impressive enough but on top of all that she lived with me while I was writing this book. There ought to be a medal for that sort of devotion.

I would also like to thank my friend Tim Stout for giving me the run of his extensive library and letting me keep some of his books for so long that when I reminded him that I still had one particular volume he told me that he'd been wondering what was supposed to fill the gap in his bookshelf. Without his help my researches into the details of the Holmes saga would have been far more difficult than they were.

FOREWORD

Firstly, let me say that I do not expect you to believe this story. Indeed, when you took this volume down from the bookshop or library shelf I suspect that you found it classified under 'fiction'. I do not believe that I can prove beyond doubt that the story is true, but I do believe that when you have read it and the review of the evidence that I have added you will, at least, be prepared to concede that it could be true.

I am not able to tell you how I came by the documents from which this narrative is drawn since the person who loaned them to me came by them dishonestly and is afraid of the consequences should the documents' whereabouts ever be disclosed. My own part of the story has been limited to arranging the notes, jottings and other parts of the narrative into order, dividing the whole story into chapers, adding the chapter headings and writing the final chapter, the retrospection. Where I thought that it was necessary I have added notes at the beginning of a chapter to indicate when and by whom it was written: these are obvious.

I have resisted the temptation to add footnotes. It would have been a simple matter to explain, for example, that 'toke' was a sort of coarse bread; that 'specks' were bruised and damaged fruits that were sold off cheaply; that Miss Morstan was destined to become Mrs Watson. But there are no footnotes in the original case-histories, and I have tried in all things to follow the originals. To those readers who are familiar with the originals and who fancy that they detect differences between them and this book, I would point out that all of the previously-published case-histories have been written up into a cohesive whole by Watson and edited by Conan Doyle: this book has not. The nearest comparison between this book and the published stories is with Chapter 10 of *The Hound of the Baskervilles* where there is an 'Extract from the Diary of Dr Watson', but, even here, it is not possible to say how much the extract has been re-worked for publication.

As I have said, I cannot prove conclusively that the story is true –

I can only say that, having spent a great deal of time researching and checking the details of the story, I believe that it is as true as any of the previously published case histories from the pen of Dr Watson or Mr Holmes.

The Mycroft Memoranda

CHAPTER 1

A Parcel from Hell

Being an extract from the diary of Dr John H. Watson, commencing on Saturday, the 20th of October 1888.

20th October A natural bohemianism of character, formed during a boyhood spent in the Antipodes and strengthened by my spell in the army, ensures that it is no hardship for me to travel; and awakening in a strange bed holds no terrors for me. So it was no maudlin sense of homecoming that made me look down into the familiar stretch of street beneath our windows with such pleasure, to watch the hard, bright sunlight flicker as the clouds scudded about the sky. It was neither the view nor the weather that cheered my spirits; I would have been as pleased to look out upon some grimy factory half obscured by driving rain or some East End alley filled with rubbish festering under a midsummer sky. Any view, in fact, that was not of the grim, grey banks of fog rolling like some monstrous beast over the sodden Devonshire moors. I had had my fill of those grim moors with their hidden secrets and dark mires, and the terrible events of the night before last were still too fresh in my mind for me to consider the countryside in any but the least favourable light.

'I'm glad to see that your wound is no longer troubling you.'

I turned to find Sherlock Holmes seating himself at the breakfast table. His thin features twitched into a smile as he caught sight of my expression. 'You appear somewhat disconcerted, Watson,' he said. 'I would suppose that you are surprised to see me up and about so early and puzzled that I know that your old wound has been troublesome of late.'

13

'Indeed,' I answered somewhat stiffly, 'I must confess myself a little puzzled, I do not make a habit of announcing to the world that my shoulder still pains me from time to time, and I am frankly baffled that you can tell that it has been by observing the manner in which I glance out of the window.'

'I deduce that your wound has been troubling you by observing the way in which you do *not* glance out of the window,' returned Holmes. 'As soon as I set eyes upon you outside the hut on the moors I could see that you were suffering more pain than is usual in your shoulder; you were somewhat more pale and haggard than is normal for you. I observed the dark scowl with which you greeted the dank mist of the moors each morning. Today, I find you regarding the sunshine with a smile more suited to the photographer's studio than the breakfast table. From these observations I surmise that the damp troubles your wound and the Devonshire mist has been the cause of considerable discomfort to you recently but that today, because of the change in the weather, you anticipate that your suffering will be relieved.'

'You have the right of it,' I said. 'As always, the trick seems less wonderful when you know how it is done.'

'It is no trick, Watson,' said Holmes. 'Come and breakfast. We will be receiving a visitor shortly, unless I miss my guess.'

'There was a letter awaiting your return, then?' I asked as I sat down at the table.

'All the letters that arrived during our absence had already been forwarded to me via Cartwright and yesterday's post was more than ordinarily dull.'

I sipped at my coffee and asked, 'Then why do you suppose we will be having a visitor?'

'When we arrived outside last night, whilst you were paying the cabbie, I took a look round. There were a number of people waiting outside the underground station across the road, but this was only to be expected. When we got inside and you were turning up the gas I noticed two men take an immediate interest and as soon as they had confirmed that we had indeed returned one made off with all haste while the other appeared to be settling down for a long wait. I was puzzled. I am engaged on no matter of importance at the moment and, though I have enemies, I could think of nobody who would benefit particularly from my demise. Nonetheless, the idea of some assassin lurking almost at my threshold was not one I relished. I stood smoking a pipe for ten minutes at the window to see if his intentions were lethiferous. . .'

'That was a risk you should not have taken,' I cried. 'What would have happened had he taken a pot at you?'

'He would have broken the mirror on the door of my wardrobe,' said Holmes with a thin smile. 'Having decided that the watcher's intentions were not hostile, I began to wonder what it was he wanted. I decided that the best way of trying to find out would be to talk to him.'

'Why did you not call on me?' I asked bitterly. 'Is it that you don't have confidence in me?'

'You know that that is not the case. If I had thought that there was any danger I would have called upon you in the instant. However, there was no danger. The watcher never even suspected that the trinket salesman who spent twenty minutes with him complaining at the lack of trade "up west" was the man he was supposed to be watching. I learned that he was a policeman in plain clothes. It takes more than a set of holiday clothes and a copy of *The Pink 'Un* to disguise one of Henry Smith's boys. What I cannot imagine, however, is why the City Police should be watching me.'

'But if they are just watching you,' I asked, 'why do you anticipate a visit in the near future?'

'Because they are no longer watching me,' he said. 'I have checked the road opposite thoroughly and nobody is keeping an eye on us. What does that suggest to you, Watson?'

'That they no longer have any interest in you?' I ventured.

'I fear that that is too optimistic a conclusion,' said Holmes, pushing his plate aside and reaching for his pipe. 'I rather think that, having assured themselves that we have returned, they have simply reported this fact to their superiors. I only hope that whatever is afoot it provides some diversion. Whatever is to follow the affair of the Hound will have to be a pretty problem indeed to avoid seeming a mere anti-climax. If you have finished eating, let's take our coffee over to the fire and see if the papers give any clue as to what has captured the interest of the men from Old Jewry.'

Almost an hour later, having scanned all the papers and consigned them one by one to the heap on the floor, Holmes pulled out his watch and gave a snort. 'I begin to think, Watson, that I may have miscalculated. It does not seem – Ah!'

He sprang up out of his armchair and over to the window. After peering out for a moment he began to chuckle. 'A hansom, Watson, pulling up outside. What does it hold for us, I wonder?' He looked out of the window again and began to rub his hands in glee. 'I am encouraged. If it were not enough to have Acting City Commissioner, Major Henry Smith visit us on a Saturday morning there is the fact that he has come here in a hansom, a mode of transport which, by all accounts, he loathes and would normally avoid. Something's up, Watson, something's up.'

Holmes came back to the fire. He found himself a cigarette from the mantelpiece, lit it and stood drawing on it impatiently while our visitor was being escorted upstairs. Eventually the boy brought him in and effected his introduction. Holmes strode across the room and held out his hand. Major Smith took it and began to apologise for intruding upon Holmes's Saturday.

'Please do not concern yourself upon that score,' Holmes replied. 'I have nothing very pressing to do today but I have every hope that you will alter that. Pray take a seat and let me furnish you with refreshment of some sort. The coffee in the pot is quite fresh, or we have something a little stronger, if you would prefer.'

'Coffee would be most agreeable, thank you,' said Major Smith.

While Holmes proffered cigarettes and cigars and I poured the coffee I took the opportunity to examine our visitor. He was a man of average size, perhaps a little older than myself, with

16

the lean, tanned look of a countryman. His face was open and cheerful and his manner friendly. Not at all what one would expect from the man who had been running the City police force for the previous six years or so. When he was settled in the armchair that Holmes had vacated to peer out of the window such a short time before, Holmes came directly to the point.

'Perhaps you will be good enough to explain to me, Major, why you have had men watching my rooms.'

Our visitor looked somewhat shamefaced at that. He gave a rueful smile and said, 'The stories I have heard of you, Mr Holmes, seem to be true. I've been trying to speak to you since Wednesday morning. We were told that you were away engaged upon a case. I've had men watching your rooms with orders to tell me as soon as you returned. When you came back last night I decided that it was too late to call on you then. Which is why I've come this morning. I hope I've not called too early and interrupted your breakfast.'

'On the contrary,' replied Holmes, 'I had expected you somewhat sooner. In what way can I be of service to the City police?'

Major Smith put down his cup and dabbed his moustache with his handkerchief. 'You will be aware, Mr Holmes, of the recent series of murders in the East End. You may be aware that there has been a development in the past few days.'

'Good Lord!' I cried. 'You mean that there has been another atrocity?'

'Mercifully, no,' replied our visitor. 'But we have received a letter which we believe has come from the murderer.'

'But surely there have been other letters? Were they not published as a poster?' I asked.

'Indeed,' agreed Major Smith. 'You refer to the letter and the postcard sent in the name of Jack the Ripper.'

'A nice touch, that,' commented Holmes absently.

'Really, I fail to see anything pleasant in it.'

'Not pleasant, Major,' said Holmes readily, 'but apposite. If the murderer's intention was to arouse the sensations of fear

17

and loathing then his *nom de guerre* is surely chosen with some skill. A letter subscribed with the name of "Eric the Disemboweller" would provoke mirth, not horror.'

'You believe the letters to have come from the criminal, then?' asked the policeman.

'I am not sufficiently aware of the facts of the case to wish to venture an opinion,' said Holmes, 'save to say that, as I recall, there was nothing in the letter or the card that might not have been written by the man you seek.'

'Do you mean to say that you know the man, Mr Holmes?' Major Smith looked somewhat disconcerted, as though he was aware that he was the butt of a joke the point of which eluded him.

'Not the man, Major Smith, but the type. This kind of motiveless and savage butchery, whilst almost unknown in England, is certainly not singular on the Continent. In Schmidt you may read the details of Stuller's crimes – he ripped open a series of women, most of whom were with child – and there are superficial similarities with the case of the Bavarian, Bichel. No doubt my cross-reference would produce other histories. However, you came not to discuss history, Major, but to speak of recent developments: a new letter?'

'Not only a letter,' said Major Smith, 'but a parcel as well.'

He stood up and took from his pocket a small parcel wrapped in brown paper. Holmes took the package from his outstretched hand and, whilst he deftly unwound the paper from the parcel, the policeman spoke again.

'It is perhaps the most gruesome clue that I have ever received.'

Holmes looked inside the package, wrinkled his nose and passed it to me saying, 'This is rather more in your line, Watson. What do you make of it?'

I opened the package, somewhat gingerly I must confess, and found inside a small, dried-up piece of offal that I recognised at once with a thrill of horror as a human kidney. I regarded it closely. It had, I could see, been put into spirits within a few hours of having been removed from the body and although it had been taken only recently, between two and three weeks unless my training had been sadly squandered, it was in an advanced state of some disease. It still had appended to it a portion of the renal artery. I could tell little more without having the opportunity of examining it further in the laboratory. I made my findings known to the others.

Major Smith produced a sheet of paper from another pocket of his jacket and asked me, 'Do you know Dr Openshaw, the Pathological Curator of the London Hospital Museum?'

'By reputation only,' I replied, 'but if what you have there is his report then I am prepared to accept his conclusions even without seeing the second opinion that he undoubtedly submitted along with it.'

'You are right to do so,' said the policeman. 'Both Dr Openshaw and a Dr Reed, from whom a second opinion was solicited, agree with your conclusions and go a little further. The kidney is, apparently, in the latter stages of Bright's disease: what is commonly known as a "ginny" kidney. This condition exactly matches that of the kidney in the body of the Mitre Square victim.'

'Kidney?' I queried.

'Yes, Doctor, only one kidney was left: the other had been removed. The murderer had sliced it out with his knife and taken it away with him.'

I was silent, a little awed at the thought of a man so demented that he could pause in the middle of laying open a body like a carcass in a butcher's shop to take out an internal organ which, hidden as it is under its layer of fat, would need steady hands and a cool brain to find, much less remove.

'You spoke of a letter, Major,' said Holmes.

'Indeed. It accompanied the kidney and was sent to Mr George Lusk, who, as you may know, is one of the founder members of the Whitechapel Vigilance Committee. Here it is.'

The note, which was in handwriting so appalling as to make the previous postcard look like a copy book, ran as follows:

Mr. Lusk   From hell
   Sir
   I send you half the Kidne I took from one woman
prasarved it for you tother piece I fried and ate it was
very nise I may send you the bloody knif that took it
out if you only wate a whil longer.
   signed Catch Me when
        you Can
        Mishter Lusk.

'I see our Jack has abandoned his trade name,' was the only comment my friend made on reading this most extraordinary communication.

'If you should agree to assist us, Mr Holmes, I have a constable downstairs with an abstract of our files on the murder of the woman whose kidney I believe this to be,' Major Smith gestured at the cardboard box, 'which is the only murder to have occurred within the jurisdiction of the City of London police, and a paste-book of newspaper pages concerning the other murders; since Scotland Yard has chosen not to take us into its confidence.

'You will then have all the information that it is within my power to give you, Mr Holmes,' said our guest, speaking with great urgency. 'Please use all your powers and give me some clue that I may set my people to following. I have done all that I can thus far. Even before the murder occurred within the City I had more than a third of my men in plain clothes loitering round the gin palaces and coffee houses, listening to the talk and slanting the conversations towards the mystery and following up any lead that might be forthcoming. And we have got nowhere. We have received all these communications and cannot even agree amongst ourselves as to which of them, if any, may have come from the fiend himself. I am at my wit's end, Mr Holmes. I believe that I have the honour to serve in the finest police force in the world and yet upon every hand we have drawn a complete blank. I beg of you, if you can throw some sort of light upon this affair, please do so.'

Holmes went over to the policeman and put a hand upon his shoulder. 'Please believe me when I say that I will do all in my power to aid you but I fear that it will not be enough.' Major Smith began to say something but Holmes interrupted him. 'What I mean is that we are dealing with a madman: not a drooling maniac, to be sure, but a man who is clearly not sane. I doubt that there is any way in which I may understand the thinking of such a person and so, I fear, the only way he may be apprehended is if he is caught in the act. With no motive to work from we shall have to rely upon luck.'

'And that has been in short enough supply of late,' said the Major sadly.

'May I ask you, Major, why you have chosen to seek my aid in this case when there have been a number of unsolved crimes in your bailiwick in the past and you have preferred to leave them unsolved rather than call upon me?'

Major Smith gave a sigh before replying. 'I have already said that I consider the City police force to be the best in the world and my detective officers are fine men; efficient, dedicated and straight runners all. I back my men with my reputation every day, and am happy to do so. I have faith in them and they know it. In the past I have considered that whilst consulting you would have probably resulted in the clearing up of some of the mysteries it would also have demoralised my men by causing them to think that I had lost confidence in them.'

Holmes had nettled slightly as the policeman had spoken of 'probably' clearing up 'some' of the mysteries, but all he asked was, 'And now?'

'Now? Now this lone madman is publicly laughing at my police force. He writes sneering letters daring us to catch him if we can – and we can't. He has even scrawled on a wall in chalk a message so ambiguous that we cannot agree whether it accuses or exculpates the Jews to whom it refers. Single-handed this fiend is destroying the police force. Street Arabs who would once have run at the sight of a constable now follow them in the street jeering at them and asking if they've caught the murderer yet. The respect that the criminal masses used to feel for my officers is disappearing. You have been a military man, Doctor, have you not?' the Commissioner asked, turning to me. I nodded and he went on, 'Well, have you seen a regiment that, through some fault or other, has failed in some endeavour? The officers and men lose faith in themselves and in their regiment. It is very rare for such a regiment to regain its spirit. It is usually disbanded.'

The Major turned back to Holmes and said, 'I will do everything I can to prevent that happening to my force. I have told my officers that I am coming to see you, indeed, prior to making the decision to come I held a meeting with my senior officers and told them that it was in my mind to consult you and asked them if they could give me any serious reason why I should not do so. Apart from a little hurt pride they gave me none.'

'Thank you, Major Smith,' said Holmes, offering his hand, 'for your candour. I say again that I will do everything I may to aid you.'

The policeman said his goodbyes and took his leave. Holmes took himself a fresh cigarette and began pacing to and fro before the fire. Eventually he caught sight of my face and stopped. 'Come on, Watson, out with it. You've obviously got something to say.'

'You said to Major Smith that our only chance of catching the fiend was to take him red-handed since there was no motive to the crimes. I recall that you once said to me that, no matter how obscure and trivial it might seem to us, there is always a motive and it is important enough to the criminal to provoke the crime. I thought I would remind you of your statement.'

'That's the devil of having a biographer,' scowled Holmes. 'You are never allowed a mistake.' Then his scowl deepened and he went back to his pacing.

CHAPTER 2

The Scene of the Crime

Holmes's scowl was still in place an hour later and, seeing that it had no intention of leaving, I decided that it would be in my interest to remove myself for what was left of the day. I knew Holmes too well to wish to stay.

This is in no way to be taken as a criticism of my friend's character, merely as my conviction, as a medical man, that his method of contemplation would be the death of me. Already the cigarettes had been cast aside and a vast quantity of venomous-looking shag had been loaded into his favourite pipes; the boy had been despatched to Long Acre to obtain whatever street maps of the area in which the murders had occurred were to be had and the files had been ransacked in an effort to find a parallel to the present series of outrages. When Holmes snapped the last of his filing drawers shut I knew that his next action would be to reach for his first pipe and that it was time for me to go. I once visited Coalbrookdale and watched one of the mighty furnaces being tapped and I would rather stand again in that foul, begrimed Gehenna of oily smoke and drifting soot than I would stay to the end of the second pipe – much less the third.

As I emerged from my room, whither I had retired to don coat and boots, Holmes looked up as though noticing for the first time that I had quit the chair by the window where I had been sitting prior to my resolution to leave. He watched in silence as I put on my overcoat and reached for my hat. As I turned towards the door he spoke.

'You have forgotten the slice of bread, my boy.'

I thanked him and moved to the table where the remains of

our breakfast still lay – Mrs Hudson would never intrude when Holmes was with a client and, after Major Smith had left, she had put her head into the room, caught sight of Holmes's scowl and retired to await a more propitious time – and was half-way through sawing off a slice before the import of his words struck me.

'How on earth did you know that I would have need of the bread?' I asked.

'You are a creature of habit, Watson. When you can no longer tolerate my company you seek respite in one of a very few alternatives. Since it is too early for billiards or the theatre and you have resisted the attractions of your club, you intend to take a turn or two around a park; and, since you always pick a park with water in it, you will undoubtedly stop to feed the ducks: hence your rather obvious need for an appropriate comestible.'

'Your reasoning is correct, of course,' I confessed, 'but how did you know that I was not going to my club?'

'If it were not enough that I can see that you have your opera glasses in one pocket and your cigar case in the other – the glasses you would not need at your club though you might want them to watch the birds and your club carries an excellent line in panatellas so you would not need to take your own – there is the matter of your "Penang lawyer".'

'But I have not brought my cane with me,' I protested.

'Just so,' said Holmes. 'Since it is your custom always to carry a stick I suppose that you intend to pick up the umbrella from the stand downstairs. You would not need protection from the rain in the lounge of your club. So, again the only conclusion is that you are heading for a time in the open.'

He was right on all counts and I could not keep the admiration out of my voice as I said, 'Holmes, you are wonderful. The more often I see your reasoning the more often I find it amazing almost to the point of unbelievability.'

The scowl, which had left his face briefly at my words, returned and he said darkly, 'You flatter me. This is but a parlour trick – *un divertissement*. But when it comes to the real work, as in the problem that Major Smith has brought us, I am the veriest beginner. I have given over an hour's thought to the problem and find myself no further forward than when I began. That is not wonderful, Watson: that is intolerable.'

'You must give yourself time, Holmes,' I said as gently as I could. 'Your mind has to sift the facts before it can produce theories to fit them. Occupy yourself with your violin and let your mind work unhampered by your own impatience.'

'Perhaps you are right,' he said. 'Enjoy your constitutional.'

He turned and walked over to where the violin rested on the cupboard beside the window, picked up the bow and began to tighten it. I doubt that he even noticed me leave.

My walk unfolded much as Holmes had predicted that it would. I walked to St James's and there sat and threw my crumbs to those avian collectors who came close enough to catch them. I tried to turn the mystery of the crimes over in my mind but found myself unable to do so. Prior to leaving Baker Street I had glanced through the paste-book Major Smith had left. Its contents had appalled me. The newspaper reports of the actual murders had been gruesome enough, with the sensationalised accounts of the circumstances of each outrage, but the inquest reports were infinitely worse, taking an almost ghoulish delight in the pathological details of the crimes. And then there were the mortuary photographs. Surrounded as I was by the beauties of nature, even subdued by the onset of winter, I found it impossible to believe that these things could be real. The trees, the reeds, the grass, the birds all seemed incontrovertible evidence of some higher agency that had set the world in order and I could not but think that such an agency would never permit such outrages as we had been told of to occur. Eventually, my metaphysics – and my bread-crumbs – exhausted, I turned my footsteps back towards Baker Street.

As I climbed the steps to our rooms I felt a moment of anxiety. What sort of a mood would I find Holmes in, I wondered. If he became depressed over his failure to solve a case that, frankly, I considered impossible, might he not seek that solace that came via the hypodermic? As a medical man, I deplore dependence on any substance but I have to admit that Holmes can put aside his apparent addiction whenever he is engaged upon a case that presents to him those curious features that he so loves. Of late Holmes had had more than his share of cases so full of the touches of the *outré* that he desired that I feared any matter that could be termed mundane would raise no enthusiasm in his breast. From the Bishopsgate Jewel Case to the Hound of the Baskervilles Holmes had had a run of unbroken triumph such as I had not seen in all the years during which I had been honoured to act as his companion. What would be the outcome if this tide of success were to break against the promontory of failure whereon stood our letter-writing madman? I hoped that Holmes had conceived of some manner in which we could lay Jack by the heels.

The scene that met my eyes as I entered our living-room was one out of an Arabian Nights fantasy. The coiling tendrils of smoke from Holmes's pipe twined sinuously around one another like a pool full of water snakes and in the midst of all sat Holmes, pulling on his old briar for all the world like an Oriental potentate with his hookah. His heavy lidded eyes flickered towards me as I entered and a smile twitched at his lips as he watched me take my kerchief from my sleeve and hold it to my mouth and nose.

'I see that you are still no fonder of the aroma of my shag,' he said with a chuckle.

'That you can see at all through this poisonous haze,' I coughed, 'is a source of wonder to me. Let us raise the sash, for pity's sake.'

'As you like,' he said with a wave of his hand that set the smoke to dancing. I took off my hat and waved it about vigorously in front of me, advancing step by step into the clearing thus formed. In a few moments I was at the window and lost no time in throwing up the bottom halves. I kept my hat in my hand and waved it with a will until I could see the far wall of the room: or could have, had I had recourse to the opera glasses.

'Have you reached any conclusions concerning the murders of which Major Smith told us?' I asked my friend as I began to divest myself of my coat.

'I have often said it is a capital error to theorise upon insufficient data,' said Holmes with some impatience, 'and, in this case, the data are so insufficient as to be non-existent. Therefore, I must have more data.' He pulled some papers from his dressing-gown pocket and glanced at them, summarising their contents to me. 'But, where to obtain these additional data? There's the rub. Athelney Jones lies racked upon his sick-bed in the grip of some fever caught as he stalked a gang of Lascar slavers across the marshes at Leigh. Lestrade continues to squelch about the mires of Devonshire, "tying up the loose ends" as he puts it, of the Baskerville case and Gregson is out of town this weekend and unobtainable until Monday. So since I am not able to get more information concerning the murders themselves I shall use the time to gain a greater knowledge of the locations in which those murders occurred. I have examined such plans as are available for the Whitechapel district and precious few there are. It would appear that while our cartographers are only too pleased to show us the course of such thoroughfares as The Mall and Birdcage Walk the meaner streets, such as Flower & Dean Street or Thrawl Street, are to them a *terra incognita*. Their attempts to show these lesser roadways are about as effective as those of the medieval mapmakers who covered the greater part of their work with the words "Here be Dragons".'

'You propose to visit the scenes of the crimes, then,' I said as I hung up my coat. 'In view of the reputation those areas have, that were a risky undertaking, surely?'

'And yet I fear it must be done. If I cannot yet understand our murderer I can at least attempt to understand his compatriots and his victims. Are you game, Watson?'

'You knew the answer ere ever you posed the query,' I said taking up my coat again. 'You'll pardon me if I take the time to return my cigars and glasses to their proper places and to fetch my stick,' I said, making for my own door.

Holmes stood clad in his Inverness when I returned and his eyes twinkled as he said, 'I see that you have decided not to rely upon your stick alone.'

I was startled for, though he was right in that I had brought my Bulldog, I had taken the trouble to slip it into my tail pocket where he could not possibly have seen it since I had faced him from the time I had come back into the room. 'Are you omnipresent now, Holmes,' I said, 'that you can see behind my back whilst you stand in front of me?'

'Perhaps I should not have said that I see,' he said with a smile, 'since it was my olfactory sense that gave me the clue. You could not disguise that gun oil of yours though you covered it with all the Sabean odours of Araby, as Milton might have said had he had less time at his disposal. Come along, Watson, though they will not be by any means Sabean, I fancy we will soon have more odours than enough.'

There was no cab to be seen as we quit the house, indeed, we had to walk as far as the Marylebone Road before we were able to hail one but we were soon on our way. Had I been some visitor from the Americas I could not have taken a better tour of the sights of the City. Our cab clattered along Baker Street and turned into Oxford Street and thence to Trafalgar Square by way of Regent Street and the Haymarket. I watched out of the window avidly; I had naught else to do. I had hoped that Holmes might share with me his first thoughts on the latest outrage but as we rode he maintained a complete silence, sitting with his eyes closed and his head sunk upon his breast as though he were asleep. As the cab trundled into the square dedicated to England's premier naval hero's greatest victory I could scarce repress a gasp at the beauty of the scene.

The fountains played jets of water into the ornamental pools, some droplets catching the late sunshine and flashing like gemstones; children thronged the place throwing crumbs for the flocks of pigeons and sparrows that floated about like the smoke from a stationary railway engine on a blustery day; Landseer's great cats lolled superiorly at their ease and, above all, the finest sailor in history looked down with, I am certain, a justifiable pride. I could not understand how Holmes could be so unmoved by it all.

'Do you not feel the loveliness of this place, Holmes?' I cried. 'Why, those fountains appear to gush the contents of the Kimberley Mines.'

Holmes's eyes flicked open and he regarded me steadily for a few seconds. 'This square is peaceful enough now,' he said slowly, 'but do not forget that it is less than two years since it was filled with a hundred thousand unemployed gathered to listen to some Irish scrivener and the Besant woman. They needed three hundred Life Guards with fixed bayonets to prevent trouble that day.'

'Anarchists and rabble-rousers,' I snorted. 'There are always idlers around who will seize upon any chance of trouble.'

'Oh, come now, Watson,' said my companion sharply, 'the labouring classes are not all idlers by any means. They are shabbily treated and it is little wonder that they turn and snap at the hand that holds them down.'

'Holmes, this is revolution!' I cried, shocked.

'Not revolution, Watson,' he said, 'merely reality. Consider. Would you expect your pug to remain faithful if you rewarded his every act with the toe of your boot? You would not. Why then expect a man to abide such treatment? And remember that every dog must have its day; as neither Borrow nor Kingsley quite said. But it was never your habit to dwell upon the wider issues but to concentrate on the minutiae. So, what thought have you had concerning the recent visit to our rooms of the Commissioner for the City of London police force?'

'Few enough, in all truth,' I said. 'This business of the kidney gives me pause.'

'It has not been definitely established that the kidney sent to Mr Lusk had been taken from the body of the last victim; though the probability is that it was,' said Holmes, his eyes gleaming.

'That is immaterial,' I said, 'since I was referring to the organ that had been removed. The very fact of its removal disturbs me.'

29

'Insanity, save when it moves into the horrifying or the humorous, is always disturbing.'

'Indeed, but you miss my point,' I said with some feeling. It was not often that I had to explain something to Mr Sherlock Holmes. 'I was considering the sort of man who could cut open a body, locate an internal organ that is by no means obvious, remove the same and still find time to notch both her ears, as the police reports state, all in less than fifteen minutes if we are to believe the evidence of the constable whose beat passes through the square.'

'Less than that,' said Holmes. 'Firstly, the killer had to give the policeman time enough to get out of earshot of any slight cry that the victim might make – and patrolling policemen are not noted for their speed – and secondly, he had to kill the woman and throw her to the ground before he could begin his atrocities. When you also consider that he had to finish and be gone before the constable returned, the time available for the mutilations shrinks to something around ten minutes. Fast work, Watson, fast work.'

Holmes's face grew grim as he spoke and I caught the glint of determination in his eye, but he did not speak again until we had arrived at the entrance to Mitre Square from Mitre Street. We paid the cabbie and listened to the rattle of the wheels across the cobbles as the cab turned about and disappeared back into Aldgate. Holmes walked rapidly into the square, turned a complete circle to orientate himself then stood looking at the south corner. Although it was not yet four o'clock in the afternoon I fancied that the square seemed dark already, but it was merely the effect caused by the sun going down – the north side of the square still had the sun upon it while the opposite side was in shadow. It was an eery effect and it was not lessened when Holmes pointed to the darkest corner and said, 'Against those wooden gates, that is where the body was discovered.'

He cast about the square again, his keen eyes flashing and his brow creased in concentration. I wondered that he did not produce his lens and creep about upon his knees, and was about to query this when I realised that a veritable horde of morbid sensation-seekers must have trooped back and forth across the ground since the deed had been done and so no clue was left to be discovered. With that thought I came to wonder why Holmes had come here at all. He was not one to visit a place solely out of morbid curiosity.

'Why have you come here, Holmes?' I asked. 'There can surely be little to interest you now.'

'The location, Watson, does that not say something to you of the character of the murderer?'

'Only that he is foolhardy in the extreme,' I commented, 'since he has chosen to commit his crime in a place where there are three entrances.'

' And how is that foolhardy?' asked Holmes with a smile.

'Why, it increases the chances of somebody coming into the square,' I answered.

'But does it not also increase the chance of somebody getting out of the square?' countered Holmes. 'Surely your military service taught you the wisdom of keeping open a line of retreat? Here our friend has secured for himself two lines of retreat, since it is unlikely that any would approach by more than one way at a time.'

I sensed that he was mocking me but, since I could see that he was right, I said nothing. The foolhardiness of launching a murderous attack in such an open location, however, struck me so forcefully that I made a small sketch, which is reproduced below, in order that I should fully comprehend the lie of the land.

'To return to the question of the removal of the kidney,' said my companion as he began to cast his eyes around the square, 'do you not find the position where the body was found significant in relation to the lamps?'

'I see no particular significance in the fact that a murderer should choose the darkest corner available in which to commit his crime,' I answered.

'But not just any murderer,' cautioned Holmes. 'A murderer who intended to cut open his victim, strew her entrails about

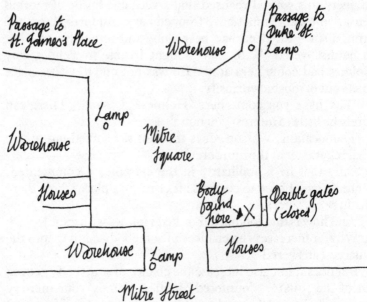

Passage to
St. James's Place

Warehouse

o

Passage to
Duke St.
Lamp

Lamp
o

Mitre
Square

Warehouse

Houses

Body
found
here ⟶ X

Double gates
(closed)

Warehouse

Lamp
o

Houses

Mitre Street

the footway and take out a part of her anatomy. Would you
attempt to do that without a light? Or with your back to the only
light that was available? And as far away from that light as you
could get? Especially when moving just a few yards along this
wall would have brought you opposite this lamp where its light
is brightest and where the lamp on the corner of Mitre Street
was also able to cast its light? There has been much speculation
in the columns of the papers as to whether the murderer has
any real anatomical knowledge and, having seen how he
spurned the use of lamps when such were readily available, I
must conclude that he was sure enough of his own ability not
to need such trivialities as a sight of what he was doing. Our
Jack works by touch alone.'

I considered my friend's words and I did not like the
implications of what he said. 'In the Afghan campaign I saw
some field surgeons whom I considered to be past masters at
their art. Men who could amputate a limb or cut out a Jezail
bullet within minutes, as they had to when the only treatment

32

for the patient other than the knife is a cup of spirit and a leather upon which to bite. None of them could have done what this fiend has done: not in the same time and in darkness.'

'Then we have learned something from this visit,' said Holmes carefully. 'Our man has some medical skill and considerable anatomical knowledge.'

'And where does this learning lead us?' I asked.

'Not all knowledge is immediately of apparent value,' he replied. 'We have learned a fact and we will remember it. Later it may become important or it may not; our next data will determine that. But, now we must be off.'

'Back to Baker Street?' I enquired.

'Hardly, my dear fellow,' said Holmes. 'We must venture into those areas to which our mapmakers are loath to go. I suggest that we quit the square by Church Passage, turn into Duke Street and thence to Whitechapel High Street by way of the Aldgate.'

CHAPTER 3

The East End

I had been into the East End before – more than once, I might add – but I could never feel at ease in those grimy streets and gloomy courts any more than I could have relaxed in the backstreets of the native townships that I visited in the bandit country of Afghanistan. Indeed, the comparisons were marked. There was the same feeling of being a stranger, a foreigner. Of feeling that one did not belong and was not welcome.

If Holmes felt the same way he gave no sign of it. As we went deeper into the slums of Whitechapel he seemed to grow more commanding, his stature seemed to increase and his countenance took on a more determined air. Watching him I was reminded of a cat from the alleys, straying out of its own area into the territory of another. The swaggering gait and the aspect of disdain were identical. They were also necessary.

Hitherto, my visits to Whitechapel and Spitalfields had been as a physician and even the vicious and bitter outcasts who inhabited these districts respected the man of medicine. Where a policeman or even a churchman might have found the way blocked there might a doctor readily find ingress. But now I was here as a civilian and though my Bulldog had never let me down I would have been tempted to exchange it for my doctor's bag – until I recalled that popular conjecture put a Gladstone into the hand of the fiend we were hunting.

By now we had come to the end of Aldgate and had begun to walk along the Commercial Road. Berner Street, the scene of the murder that immediately preceded the crime in Mitre Square, was, as I recall, the second on the right. We turned into it and after only a few paces Holmes stopped and said, 'If the newspaper reports are to be believed, we are now standing at the spot where the body was discovered: here, at the end of this yard.'

I glanced into the yard and almost expected to see the woman still lying there. There was, however, nothing to see save the cobbles and the windows. I tried to look at this site in the way that Holmes had looked at the other and immediately a question sprang to my lips.

'If what you said about lines of retreat was true for the other site, Holmes, how is it that on this occasion the fiend appears to have selected a dead end in which to commit his crime?'

'Bravo, my boy. I wondered if you would see that,' said Holmes warmly. 'I can but suppose that he knew this yard and thought that it would be empty for the few minutes he would require. It must have been a considerable shock to him when the carter turned his horse into it. Perhaps that shock is what made him pick such an open site as the square for his next attempt. Who can tell?'

Holmes's voice trailed off as he began a minute examination of the yard. Although he again eschewed the use of his lens, Holmes paced up and down until he had set foot upon practically every part of it. I could not help but notice that his interest in the yard had not gone unremarked.

'Holmes, we are observed,' I said quietly, taking a firmer hold upon my stick.

'You mean the collection of ruffians at the window along there?' he answered. 'I doubt that they will trouble us. We are two hale fellows, armed with sticks moreover, and they look as though they possess neither the physical nor mental facilities to persuade a drowning man to climb into a dory. However, I have seen all I wish to here so we may as well move along.'

'I take it you have some aim in mind,' I commented as I fell in beside him.

'Not a definite aim in the sense that I head for a particular spot,' replied Holmes. 'I merely seek to gain an impression of this region at first hand. Little crime of interest to me has been committed here. The taste here runs to simple robbery and violence for its own sake. Nothing to attract the specialist. This is the part of London that I know least and which our quarry seems to know so well.'

Had you asked me before I set out on that walk, I would have told you that I knew the East End: that I had seen its horrors and that nothing it could produce would shock me. Along with a number of my brother physicians I had given of my time to the London Hospital where we had done what we could for the poor wretches who came to the out-patients clinic. I had always travelled from Baker Street to Whitechapel on the Underground Railway, for the hospital is directly across the road from the station. I had been making those trips for the past four years or so, ever since my constitution recovered sufficiently for me to consider going back into practice again, and yet how little I had seen of the area in those four years. It is true that I had answered any number of calls to attend at the bedside (such as it usually was) of some needy person but always I had had some guide to take me through the warren of streets and alleys that lay behind the main streets. And there was always such a sense of urgency that I had had little time to notice any details of the places through which we passed. How different was it when one had time to look.

Some of the sights I saw I could not set down upon the page, not alone because they would outrage common decency, but also because I would not be believed. I saw sights too heart-rending, too infuriating, too pathetic to be credible. At the first there were the dwellings amongst which we passed. Single rooms that I would have blushed to offer a maid of all work are inhabited by whole families – and in some cases two or three generations of the family – with sometimes upwards of a dozen persons eating, sleeping and, when their release came, dying, all in the same room. And these rooms were to be had only in tenement buildings, dark, ill-kempt and verminous, connected by vile alleys full of discarded filth which open into tiny courts where the light of the sun never penetrates and the refuse festers. Upon every hand was to be seen some new horror;

mistreated children, abandoned women or dissolute men. Things such as I had never witnessed in the gold-fields of Australia or the worst slums of Bombay or the Afghan territories.

Eventually we came to a halt at the end of a short street at the other end of which a queue of bedraggled men waited at the door of some grim building. I heard Holmes's sharp intake of breath and asked, 'What is it?'

'The Whitechapel casual ward,' he replied. 'Better known to those who have to use its services as the Spike.' He took out his watch and glanced at it. 'There is still almost an hour to go before they open the doors but I'll lay odds that those men at the head of the queue have been there since one o'clock.'

'But surely,' I said, 'this gives the lie to your earlier protestations concerning the willingness of the working classes to live up to that description.' I fear that I was a little strident, but the sight of the men, some of whom were neither old nor infirm, waiting to be let in for a free night's lodging when they could have been earning the money to rent better accommodation on the open market had nettled me. 'The time that these idlers have spent waiting here could have been better spent seeking useful employment rather than worrying about where to sleep.'

'There, Watson, you betray the prejudice of one who has no fears as to the availability of his next meal or of his bed for tonight,' said Holmes slowly, 'but these poor souls have only the most precarious hope of achieving either of those comforts for this, or any other, night. I suppose that you have observed the number of poor persons who sleep at whatever spot they may during the day?'

'Indeed I have: row upon row of them, as often as not.'

'And I gauge from your tone that you have resented their daylight slumber without knowing that they are not allowed to sleep by night. They are rousted out from the parks and the railway arches and moved on by the authorities at every turn. It is not unknown for a man to be roused a dozen times during the night. Come the morning, is it any wonder that he is in no fit state to look for work? Even if he does he stands little chance of finding anything other than the most casual of work. Is it any wonder, then, that after three or four sleepless nights a man should seek either a night in the Spike or a day in the Spitalfields Garden? And once he begins he is trapped. He must either sleep all day in the Garden or work at picking oakum in the Spike to pay for his bed and toke so that he no longer has the time to seek gainful employment.'

As the meaning of what Holmes had said sank in I said, 'It is like being trapped in a mire. If one struggles one is sucked down as a result of one's endeavours whereas if one does not struggle one is drawn down just as surely if somewhat more slowly. It is a progress of despair.'

'And one which will be broken by violence if no other method is found,' said my companion thoughtfully.

I was silent for I had never thought of the things Holmes had put before me. My whole upbringing had taught me that a man should fend for himself and not look to charity and yet Holmes, whom I had always found to be a stern critic of wasters, was here defending those who applied for the most basic charity. Indeed, he was proposing that the system of charity itself was responsible for much of the needs of it. There was much here that I needed to think on. But we had other problems more immediate. As always seemed to be the case in the East End, the moment you stopped and took an interest in a scene you yourself became the object of considerable interest on the part of the local population.

'Holmes,' I said, 'at the risk of repeating myself I must point out that we are again observed. And this time by a more villainous-looking aggregation than before.'

'Fall in beside me, Watson,' he said, beginning to move towards the loafers at the end of the street, 'and we'll put their mettle to the test.'

'They are a rough-looking group,' I said as I came up beside him. 'Might they not be the Old Nichol Gang?'

'Wrong part of London,' Holmes snapped. 'I think we shall be best advised to head for the nearest main road. If we follow our noses in this direction,' he gestured with his stick, 'we shall come out into the Whitechapel Road.'

We stepped it out sharply until we reached the thoroughfare that Holmes had named. I looked back and was alarmed to see that some of the loafers were still behind us. Holmes had caught my glance.

'Yes, they are nothing if not persistent,' he commented. 'I wonder why they stick to us so?'

'That is easy enough, surely,' I said. 'We have the smell of money about us.'

'The only thing I smell about you is your revolver,' he said. 'But I wonder how we are going to escape their attentions. Whilst I am sure that you and I could acquit ourselves easily if things came to a common brawl I am loath to let that happen.'

'Why?' I asked. 'You are surely not afraid to hurt them?'

'If I must needs follow our Jack through these streets I would rather do so without a horde of vengeance-seeking toughs at my back.'

'Well, then,' I said, 'let us visit the clinic at the London and see if any of my colleagues are to be found. We can always have the porter hail us a cab when our business is done.'

Since Holmes concurred, we did as I had suggested and crossed the road. The London Hospital is, perhaps, the most imposing building in the East End. It is, without doubt, the most important. It is the only service of out-patient relief available to the citizens of the areas of Whitechapel, Spitalfields and Aldgate. In this respect it is to be regarded as more important than the great hospitals of the more prosperous regions of the capital, since they are there merely to supplement the services of the districts' doctors and clinics. For the people of the East End, however, aside from the London, there were only the barber's assistants who could remove a wart or apply a leech with more or less skill than any other quack and whose degrees from obscure foreign universities were as worthless as their prescriptions.

Holmes and I went in through the gate in the fence, narrowly avoiding being hit by a carriage coming out with more speed than was prudent for the safety of either passengers or other users of the path that led up to the main doorway. We left the path and skirted off to the right-hand doorway into the Front Block, whence we passed through that block, out through the West Wing and along the path beside the House Governor's Garden until we reached the College. We were just about to enter the main doors when they were flung open and a figure that I recognised at once strode out.

'Halloa, Doyle!' I cried. 'What are you doing up here?'

The big fellow turned from the door he had been in the act of shutting and, seeing me, gave a good-natured grunt before coming forward with a smile and outstretched hand. 'You may be sure that I did not journey all the way up from Southsea just upon the chance that I might run into you, Watson.' He seized my hand and began to work it as though it were a village pump. 'But it is good to see you again. You look wonderfully well, except for the pain lines around your eyes.'

By now I had managed to get my hand back and I used it to indicate Holmes. 'Dr Conan Doyle, Mr Sherlock Holmes,' I said.

Doyle immediately held out his hand again, 'Mr Holmes,' he said, 'what a very great pleasure to meet you.'

'I wish that I could say the same,' replied Holmes. The chuckle he gave and the speed with which he took the proffered hand robbed his words of any offence and he quickly explained his apparent rudeness. 'I believe that I have you to thank for getting Watson's scribblings into print in that infernal annual last Christmas?'

'I must confess to that,' said Doyle. 'And I believe that more accounts of your work should be made available to the public for, in that manner, people will become aware of the standards to which the practice of detection may be raised.'

'And you think that important?' asked Holmes.

'Indeed I do,' said Doyle.

'Pray tell me why,' said Holmes. I could see that Holmes was much taken with my fellow doctor and I was not greatly surprised, for Doyle was a fine specimen of young manhood.

I knew that both Holmes and Doyle were at home in the boxing ring and there is about the exponent of the noble art an air that a fellow devotee may feel and respond to. There was also a similarity in appearance, by which I do not mean that their faces were similar but that they had the same carriage and the same alert glance.

Doyle was answering Holmes's request for an explanation. 'It is my belief that the public should be aware of, and only prepared to accept, the highest standards in all the professions. It is no more than they deserve. However, you must not let me get on to this subject or I will discourse to you all day. Perhaps we may have a fuller discussion at some future date?'

'I would welcome the opportunity,' said Holmes with a deal more warmth than I would have expected. 'Here is my card. Please feel free to look me up when you are in London again. Or perhaps you will have the time during this visit?'

'Regrettably not. I must catch this evening's Portsmouth train.' Doyle lowered his voice to a conspiratorial whisper and said, 'I only got up here this time by bringing a patient up for a consultation in Harley Street.' I had been recalling the simplicity of Doyle's hospitality and wondering how his indigence had permitted him the luxury of a trip to Town. 'Still,' he said, 'the trip did give me a chance to obtain some textbooks from the Charing Cross Road and to cut across here for a quick glimpse at the library.' He patted his breast pocket and added, 'I think that I've got the answer to a case that has been puzzling me for the last month. But, perhaps you will be able to come down to Southsea in the near future. I would welcome the company. Here is my card, sir; though, I fancy, young Watson needs no prompting as to the address. Good day to you, Mr Holmes. I hope I shall see you shortly, Watson.' With that he turned and made his way towards the main building.

I could see that Holmes's curiosity had been aroused by the meeting but I knew that he would not pry into my private life by asking after the circumstances of my previous contact with Doyle. I thought it best to put his mind at rest since he needed to have it uncluttered with anything that was not directly concerned with the case in hand.

'Interesting fellow, young Conan Doyle,' I said. 'When I first arrived in England from Afghanistan I knew few people and had no family at all to whom I might turn. I was completely alone when I stepped off the troopship *Orontes* at Portsmouth jetty. I did have, however, a letter for Dr Doyle from one of the staff surgeons at Peshawar who had been at Edinburgh with him. And a deal of trouble I had trying to deliver that letter, too. At my first attempt to learn of Doyle's whereabouts I was told that he had shipped in a whaler and was sailing about the Arctic. In fact, at the time I was looking for him he was back in England but by the time I learned that he had taken ship again; this time bound for the tropics of West Africa. It was not until shortly before our visit to Stoke Moran to aid Miss Stoner that I heard that Doyle had put up his plate at Southsea. I found out his address from my medical connexions and wrote to him enclosing the letter and a note explaining the reasons for its late delivery. Doyle wrote back and invited me to look him up should I ever find myself in Southsea and at a loose end. This was at the time when you did not choose to call me in on all your cases. . .'

'My dear fellow,' interrupted Holmes, 'had the choice been left to me I should have had your aid in all of my cases. But I had your health to consider. You must recall how frangible was your constitution in those days? I could not permit you to throw too great a strain upon your strength.'

'Well,' I said, a little touched by the concern in his voice, 'that's as may be, but the fact is that I found myself with a deal of spare time upon my hands in those days. And after the excitements and exertions of the hunt for Jefferson Hope I felt that I would benefit from a short rest. I wired Doyle to say that I would be staying in his neighbourhood for a few days and suggesting that we might meet. Doyle immediately wired back saying that he had rooms to spare at his home and suggesting that I should stay there. I had no sooner arrived at his home than I succumbed to a bout of the enteric fever which, as you know, recurs at regular intervals. Doyle reclassified me from guest to patient and treated me himself.

'I stayed with him for something over a month, until I felt strong enough to make the journey back to London. I have been in correspondence with him ever since and it was he who suggested that I write up the notes I had made of the case that began as the Lauriston Gardens mystery.'

'Then he has a great deal to answer for,' observed Holmes. 'But what now? Are there people you wish to see while we are here, Watson?'

'I had nobody in mind when we came in,' I answered, 'but it occurs to me that I could use the time to check on the need for help at the clinic. Since our trip to Devonshire I am a little out of touch.'

Holmes raised no objections so we went into the library of the medical college where the list of volunteers was to be found. I was quite relieved to see that it was pretty full at the moment. I said, 'I think that, if you should wish me to, I can assist you for the next few days in your present enquiries. There does not seem to be a pressing need for a spare hand and, in any event, they have my address should they want me in a hurry.'

'If they do not need your services,' said Holmes, 'I can assure you that I do.'

Holmes's tone was a trifle enigmatic and I was not at all sure that he was not laughing at me. 'I really fail to see, Holmes, just what use I am to you in your work. I can see that you appreciate an extra gun in your hide occasionally but that is all.'

'If that were all,' said Holmes warmly, 'it would be more than enough on its own. But in my work I have to hit the gold with my first shot as often as not and that were difficult indeed on my own. You are my ranging shot, Watson; by observing where your practical common-sense leads you I may see where to concentrate my efforts. You are my forlorn hope, in the strictly military sense of the expression, of course.'

I must admit that his words gave me keen pleasure, for I had often been somewhat piqued by his apparent indifference to my attempts to help him in his work and it was with a feeling of

some gratification that I walked with him through to the main
entrance and waited until the porter had secured us a cab.

CHAPTER 4

Sir Charles Warren

21st October A Sunday. Holmes stayed in bed until well after breakfast and seemed tired and listless when he did at last emerge. He ate little and said virtually nothing throughout the day. Having failed to find solace in either his violin or his beloved chemical experiments, he went back to his card index and began to go through it with greater diligence than he had shown before. By the time we had tea sent up he had a little heap of half a dozen or so cards set to one side. When I asked him if they were his suspects in the Whitechapel murder case he nodded sadly.

'Yes, they are,' he said, 'though I have little hope that any of them will prove to be the miscreant. Ostrog has the medical knowledge and Kosminski has a known hatred of unfortunates but I doubt that there is a shred of evidence against either of them; or any of the others whose cards I have retained.'

'But you will make enquiries?' I asked.

'Naturally. It is more important to know what does not fit in with the case against a suspect than it is to know what does. However, I have done all that I may at the moment. Pass me up the papers again, my boy, and let us go through the theatre notices. It has been much too long since we were last at Covent Garden.'

22nd October A surprise at the breakfast table! Holmes was up and on to his second egg by the time I sat down. In contrast to his apparent depression of the day before – he had even appeared to sleep through the evening, though from the way he had hummed the refrains from several of the pieces in the cab afterwards, I judged that he had been paying as much attention as anybody else – he was so ebullient and cheerful that I feared that he might have had recourse to the needle during the night. His first words to me, however, partially put my mind at ease.

'Good morning, Watson,' he said. 'And I believe that it is going to be a very good morning.'

'Well, I must say that you seem in very changed spirits this morning, Holmes,' I said. 'It is wonderful what a good night's sleep will achieve.'

Holmes chuckled as he poured me a cup of coffee and said, 'My cheer this morning comes to me courtesy of the messenger service, not Morpheus. Gregson has heard that I have been asking after him and has wired to say that he will be in his office later and has reserved half an hour of his time for us at ten o'clock. I have great hopes. If there are worthwhile data to be had, Gregson will sift them for us.'

We breakfasted quickly and Holmes lingered over his coffee and the newspapeers until the time for our meeting with Gregson drew near. We had no trouble finding a cab and were soon at the main entrance to Scotland Yard.

As we paid off the cabbie Holmes glanced up at the building and remarked, 'Scotland Yard, home of the best official detective force in the world, though that's saying little enough. Still, I must admit that they are at the precise level of competence that is best for my business.'

'Why do you say that?' I asked.

'If they were very much more efficient, I should not be needed,' he said, his good humour bubbling up again, 'and if they were any less conscientious, they would not bring their problems to me for solution and I would miss some of my most interesting and instructive cases.'

By now we had made our way inside where Holmes announced our names to the officer at the desk and we were ushered into Gregson's tiny office without delay. Gregson stood up as we came into his room, the pale colouring of his office serving only to emphasise the pallor of his white face and flaxen hair and his height seeming to make the small room even more uncomfortable. However, we managed to sort ourselves out in fairly short order and were soon seated around his desk, though I fear we presented more the appearance of a conspiracy of anarchists than a consultation of policeman, detective and doctor. Holmes came straight to the point.

'Now then, Gregson,' he said briskly, 'I have come to you for a little help.'

The tall policeman gave a small laugh and said, 'I would be more than happy to be of whatever assistance I can. More often than I would care to admit to a promotion board I have had to seek your help and it has always been forthcoming. In what way may I be of help to you, Mr Holmes?'

'I should very much like,' replied Holmes, 'to run my eye over the Yard's files on the Whi—'

He got no further. The door to Gregson's office was flung open with such violence that it crashed into the back of my chair with, I felt, sufficient force to catapult me into the Inspector's lap had I not grabbed the edge of the desk with both hands. A great voice seemed to fill the room.

'What's this?' it roared. 'One of my officers in hugger-mugger with interfering busybodies, I'll be bound.'

I had by now managed to return all four of my chair's legs to the floor so I turned to look at the man who loomed through the wide-flung door. He was an average-sized man with dark hair and a moustache that looked as though it had not benefited from the edge of a razor for at least a fortnight. As to what his face would normally have looked like I could not say since, at the moment, it was of such a colour as to put a ripe tomato to shame. Holmes has not so much as flicked an eyelid, much less turned his head; he sat as though waiting for the disturbance to pass as if the interruption had been nothing more remarkable than a passing four-wheeler. This indifference seemed only to incense further our already irate visitor.

'Have you nothing to say for yourselves?' he demanded. 'Perhaps it is that you are caught out in your creeping about and can find nothing to say in your own defence. Well, if you have nothing further to discuss, I suggest that you – gentlemen –

leave. No doubt you can find your way out through whichever backway you used to insinuate yourselves in here.'

Holmes is a man of infinite patience. I have seen him hunch for hours over some chemical experiment or other, waiting uncomplainingly for some reaction or other sign that he had achieved what he wished. Discourtesy is the one thing that will rouse him, instantly and inevitably. Had there been a lady present I am convinced that Holmes would have caught the intruder a box upon the ear before he had half finished the speech I have set out above. As it was he turned and spared the newcomer a mere glance before turning back to Gregson.

'I take it that this is some new attempt to rehabilitate the criminally insane,' he said in the manner of one pointing out a new cut of suit or style of hat. 'You retain some of these fellows to amuse your visitors.'

Gregson looked acutely unhappy but he was allowed no time to speak.

'Do you not know who I am?' cried the red-faced gentleman with much surprise in his voice as though he could not believe that there could be living in the latter part of the nineteenth century any who did not know him.

'Since you waited for no introductions,' said Holmes calmly, 'but commenced your vituperations even before you had crossed the threshold it is not to be wondered at that I did not catch your name.' He stood up and presented his card. 'Allow me to introduce myself. I am Sherlock Holmes and this gentleman is Dr Watson, my colleague and my friend.'

So pleasantly had Holmes made his own introduction that the contrast between his polished urbanity and the uncouth behaviour of the other quite took the intruder aback. He seemed at a loss for a few moments until he happened to glance down at the card that Holmes had given him. His colour, that had faded from tomato to whey, now blossomed to the most violent beetroot. 'So, Mr Sherlock Holmes, eh?' he said to himself. 'Then I was right to come down. I am Sir Charles Warren, the Commissioner of the Metropolitan Police. What, may I enquire, are you doing here, sir?'

Warren had adopted an insufferably superior tone in his last two sentences and I could see that Holmes was beginning to lose the good humour he had managed to retain up to now. Holmes always stands well, never lounging unless some part he is playing demands it, but now he drew himself up even more so that he could look down upon the Commissioner. When he spoke his voice was like the rasp of a vesta across the milled edge of a matchcase.

'I had come here, Sir Charles, to offer the Yard my assistance in the clearing up of the matter of the Whitechapel horrors. It has always been my policy in the past to work only on those matters that were brought to my attention by my clients,' Holmes paused before adding, 'or Metropolitan Police officers who found themselves out of their depth. I may now say,' continued Holmes with some heat, 'that I shall not, in any way, assist or advise the Yard while it continues to have as its Commissioner a man whose inadequacy is matched only by his churlishness.'

For a moment I thought that I should have to attend upon Sir Charles in a professional capacity; I feared that he was about the throw a fit. It was not possible for him to become any redder in the face than he already was but he stood and gasped with his mouth opening and closing like a fainted man revived with a panful of iced water. After a while he seemed to recover himself.

'I'll thank you to leave, sir,' he said attempting to meet Holmes's steady gaze and not succeeding, 'before I have you forcibly removed from the premises and flung into the street where a charlatan like you belongs.'

'I shall go immediately I have said one more thing,' replied my companion. 'Gregson here had no knowledge of why I was coming to see him. You will take no action against him because of today's events.'

'By God!' roared Warren, 'am I to be told by you how I should run my commission? I will have you know, sir, that I am answerable only to Her Majesty's Home Secretary and not to every jackanape confidence trickster who conies the public into believing that he can perform that work which is best left to the official forces of the law.'

'I am aware whence your authority devolves,' said Holmes coldly. 'Just as I am aware that Henry Matthews has shielded you from much heat. But I would remind you that I am not unconnected and will not hesitate to use those connexions should any injustice be done to Gregson as a result of this fiasco. Good day, sir.'

This last was delivered over his shoulder as he sauntered out. I followed Holmes out and, as Sir Charles declined to move aside and give me sufficient room, was obliged to tread upon the policeman's boot as I did so. I fear that my protestations of apology salved neither his hurt foot nor his hurt pride. By the time I caught up with Holmes he had left the building and was stalking down the street with a face like thunder and a glint in his eye that boded ill for any unfortunate enough to impede his progress. He said not a word until he stood upon the Embankment. For a period of several minutes he stared at the traffic moving up and down the great artery that carries the largest amount of cargo to go into or come out of any port in the world. Though the great ocean-going merechantmen were compelled to dock below London Bridge, the sight of the barges and lighters seemed to relax him, as though putting the petty squabbles of individuals into a proper perspective. Eventually, Holmes gave a sigh and turned to me.

'Thank you, my dear fellow,' he said warmly.

'For what?' I queried. 'I did nothing.'

'You must not forget your attack upon the Commissioner,' replied Holmes with a chuckle.

'That was his own fault,' I said, though I could not resist a smile. 'He would not allow me enough space to pass.'

'Did you know that he had a corn upon the foot you crushed?'

'Indeed I did not,' I said. 'How on earth did you know?'

'By the toe-cap of his boot,' said Holmes. 'The big toe tends to point upwards while the others lie flat. Thus the big toe presses upon the leather of the boot from the inside and raises a small hump. When there are two humps it is because the second has been raised by the bandage used to hold a plaster in place over a corn.'

At this I could not resist a laugh myself, until a thought struck me. 'Holmes, did you mean what you said about declining to assist the police in the future?'

'Inasmuch as I said that I would not assist the Metropolitan force while Warren remained its head, yes,' he replied.

'That is a little harsh of you, surely,' I said. 'Ultimately it will be the public who are the sufferers.'

'Indeed,' agreed Holmes. 'However, it is my conviction that Warren will not see the year out in his present position. I doubt that he would survive the outcry that would follow if there is another murder and even if there is not he has so demoralised the force that a change must be made soon. I only hope that the authorities have the sense to reinstate, and promote, Monro.'

'What do you plan to do now?' I asked.

'I suppose that we should report the signal failure of my investigations to Major Smith,' said Holmes. 'We owe him that much, at least.'

It took us but a few seconds to hail a cab and soon we were rattling our way along the Embankment, heading towards the City. We left the Embankment at Blackfriars Bridge and clattered up almost to the Mansion House, passing the beautiful College of Arms as we did so, and thence to Old Jewry by way of Queen's Street and Poultry. We paid off the cab at the junction of Poultry and Old Jewry and walked not quite to the other end until we found, upon the left-hand side, the police headquarters, hidden away in a little court. Here, however, a disappointment awaited us. When we asked for Major Smith we were told that he was not in the building nor was he expected to return until late in the afternoon. Holmes left his card and asked that the Commissioner be informed that we had been looking for him when he returned and that we would come again to the office at a time that was convenient or that Major Smith would be most welcome at Baker Street should he find that a visit there would be more amenable to him. This done we were at something of a loose end.

I was a little concerned, for I did not want Holmes to have too much time on his hands to brood about the slight that he had received from Sir Charles Warren. Holmes was a man who was proud – justifiably so – of his achievements and, like all true artists, most sensitive about any denigration of those achievements. So, something to while away the time until we should hear from Major Smith. . .? Of a sudden the solution sprang into my mind, along with a way in which I could propose it to Holmes without suggesting that it was he whose welfare I was considering.

'I seem to recall,' I said, 'that Nevill's have a place hereabouts, in Broad Street I believe. I think that a steam bath and a rub down are just what I need finally to take the mist of the Devonshire moors out of my bones. If I can prevail upon you to accompany me, Holmes, we could pass a couple of hours away and then look about for somewhere to have a spot of lunch.'

'I feel that you think I am in need of a cold plunge to get me over my meeting with Warren,' he said with a thin smile. 'But you need have no concern for me, Doctor. *Ira furor brevis est.* Horace perhaps did not know medicine but he knew men.'

The bathe, a pipe in the indolence of the drying-room and lunch so repaired Holmes's disposition that, upon our return to Baker Street, he spent the afternoon and evening poring over his files seeking, as I saw when I glanced over his shoulder, details of crimes that involved the killing and mutilating of women; especially of women of the streets. Whenever he came across a case that he considered relevant he would make a résumé of the details until he had two or three foolscap sheets covered in data. When he had completed his researches he flung down his pen, strode across the room and tugged at the bell-rope. When Mrs Hudson bustled up in response to his call, he asked if she would be so kind as to send up a pot of tea and a few pieces of her own shortbread.

'You have an exceptionally good appetite today,' I stated. 'It is unusual to get you to eat lunch and for you to eat both lunch and tea on the same day is almost unheard of.'

'You will recall that I declined a sweet in the restaurant and stuck with my pipe while you were tackling that cream and pastry concoction that you were unable to take your eyes off from the moment that you first caught sight of it on the trolley. I think my main course sufficiently digested now for me to consider a dessert. I think tea and biscuits would be most acceptable.'

As if on cue Mrs Hudson reappeared with a tray which I took from her and carried to that table adjacent to Holmes's desk. We were still waiting for the tea to infuse when we heard a ring at the bell. A few seconds later Major Smith showed himself into the room. He caught sight of the pot and cups and smiled.

'I seem to have a habit of calling when you are about your meals,' he said. 'I must apologise for inconveniencing you.'

'Not at all,' said Holmes. 'Unless I am very much mistaken Mrs Hudson will send the boy up with an extra cup and saucer for you. She has an uncanny knack of knowing whether a caller is merely a client or something more.'

He was quite correct, of course, and when the additional cup had been brought and all of us served he came to the business in hand at once.

'I am afraid, Major, that I will be unable to help you in your present predicament.'

'What do you mean?' asked our visitor anxiously.

'I mean, sir, that there are insufficient data available for me to base a conclusion upon,' replied Holmes. 'If, Heaven forfend, it should happen that there is another murder, then I will be more than willing to examine the body and the location in which that body is found in an effort to discover some clue as to the identity of the murderer. Failing that, I fear that there is little I can do.'

'Perhaps if you were able to peruse the files on the murders that occurred in the Metropolitan Police's district you might be able to see some connexion, some pattern.'

'I had thought of that, Major Smith. Dr Watson and I visited Scotland Yard this morning in an effort to do just that.'

'What happened?' asked the policeman.

'We were thrown out, almost physically I might add, by Sir Charles Warren,' answered Holmes bitterly. 'I have given him my word that I will not in any way assist the Metropolitan force while he remains as its head.'

'Mr Holmes,' cried our guest, 'I can understand your decision, but I must call upon you to reconsider. Catching the Ripper is above any petty clash of personalities, surely?'

'I wholeheartedly agree with you,' said Holmes warmly. 'That is why I will do whatever I may to help the City police find the murderer. If, in doing so, I help the Metropolitan force clear some cases from its unsolved list then that is by the by.'

'Even so,' commented Major Smith, 'to deny your help to the largest force in the country is not a course of action that I would have expected you to take, Mr Holmes.'

'Watson said just the same thing to me earlier,' replied Holmes. 'And I will tell you the same as I told him. I do not expect that Warren will see out the year as Commissioner for the Metropolitan force. His position at the moment is precarious and, in the event of another outrage, will become untenable.'

'He should never have been appointed in the first place,' said our visitor. 'Jim Monro is the obvious man for the job. Until Warren is removed from his present position the two police forces of the metropolis will never be able to act in concert. So, we must await developments, Mr Holmes?'

'I fear so, Major Smith,' agreed Holmes. 'I am sorry that I have not been able to be of more assistance to you.'

Rather to my surprise, Major Smith came to his feet with a great smile. He put down his tea cup and said, 'Ah, but you have given me the best help that you possibly could.'

I did not understand what he could possibly mean and thought that perhaps he was japing us, but Holmes smiled and said, 'You mean your men?'

'Exactly,' replied the policeman. 'they will not feel so badly about their own failure when I tell them that the great Sherlock Holmes is unable to do any better.'

'But it is unfair to compare my friend's efforts now with those of the men at the scenes of the various crimes,' I said. I was a little terse, I fear, but I did not like to see Holmes's reputation bandied about quite so casually. 'It is not a true comparison.'

'You yourself must bear the responsibility, Watson,' said Holmes. 'It was you who set me up as infallible. You cannot complain then when others take delight in my failure. Do not hesitate to call upon me should there be some significant development.'

This last was addressed to Major Smith whom Holmes was guiding to the door. The policeman assured Holmes that any news of importance would be communicated to our rooms within a quarter of an hour of its having been received at his office. With that he bade us good evening and left.

'A fine, dedicated officer,' said Holmes crossing to the window and looking out. 'I would that there were more officers of his rank who took their responsibilities as seriously as he. The difference between the calibre of Major Smith and Sir Charles Warren shows both the virtue and the drawback of having a political appointee as Commissioner. You have little idea of the sort of man you are going to get. They are either the best, like Smith, and chosen for their ability, or the worst, like Warren, and chosen because somebody wants to get into their good books.'

'But surely the Commissioner must be answerable to the Cabinet?' I said. 'And that being the case, the Cabinet is inevitably going to want to appoint its own man. The thing that bothers me, though, is what you intend to do now?'

'You need not concern yourself that I am going to sit and brood on the events of the day, even should I wish to,' said my companion with a twinkle in his eye. 'There is a brougham pulling up at the kerb and, unless I am far wide of the mark, it contains a client. If you would be so kind as to carry the tea things into your room and out of sight I'll slip out of this lounging jacket and into something rather more formal. I fancy the lady who is coming to see us is something of a stickler for the niceties.'

Watson's diary continues with a description of the meeting between Holmes and his client, Mrs Upwood, and of Holmes's investigation into the allegations that his client's son had been cheating the Nonpareil Club of considerable sums of money at cards. This case, together with the ramifications of the murder charge levelled by the French police against Mme Montpensier in connexion with the disappearance of her step-daughter, which necessitated that Holmes visited France, fully occupied the detective's attention from the 22nd of October until the 8th of November 1888, when the Whitechapel murders were again brought to Holmes's attention. The details of the two cases mentioned above have not been included since they have no bearing on the main subject of this book. They might be published at a later date.

CHAPTER 5

Whitehall by Command:
Whitechapel by Night

8th November I am often concerned over the health of my fellow lodger. At those times when he has no case to consider he succumbs to his natural lassitude and indolence and a consideration of his health has very much to take a postillion. At those times when he does have a case in hand he neglects his bodily needs even more shamefully. I have known him go three days at a stretch with only his pipe and flask to provide sustenance. As his doctor, as well as his friend, I am naturally disturbed at this cavalier treatment of his physical frame. And yet I am forced to admit, as an impartial observer, that his body does not appear to have suffered as a result of the eccentric habits of its owner. His frame, whilst not apparently very strong, is lithe and wiry, and very supple withal. I had expected that he would need a complete rest upon our return to Baker Street from France where, as part of his defence of the much maligned Mme Montpensier, Holmes had run over five kilometres of rolling countryside within a quarter of an hour in order to demonstrate to the French authorities that it might be done. But, far from wanting to rest, Holmes was in excellent spirits as he came into breakfast.

'I see you've made a good start to the day,' he said, eyeing the plates I had pushed away from my position. 'No doubt you have felt deprived during the last few days.'

'Indeed I have,' I replied. 'The French habit of beginning the day with naught more filling than a cup of coffee and a roll that is two-thirds air is not one I would wish to adopt permanently. A man needs a decent English breakfast if he is to face the vicissitudes of the day with equanimity.'

'Well, I had better hurry, then,' said Holmes, sitting down. 'I shall be receiving a visitor within the next half-hour, if his wire is to be believed.'

He would say no more until he had finished eating and had carried his last cup over to the fire. He had been eagerly looking through the papers but had failed to find what he was looking for. Eventually he threw the journals aside and tossed off the last of his coffee.

I could not help but aim a dart at him. 'You have been unable to discover what it is that your expected visitor wishes to consult you about?' I asked innocently.

'Unless they wish me to take part in Saturday's Lord Mayor's procession I am completely at a loss,' he said. 'However, I fancy that our curiosity will be allayed shortly for this is, surely, our client.'

But in his assumption Holmes was both right and wrong. The ring at the bell had indeed announced the arrival of his visitor, but it was not a client. It was a policeman. A plain-clothes Scotland Yarder.

'Inspector Fred Abberline, at your service, sir,' he said after Holmes had invited him to take a seat.

'You are undoubtedly aware of my recent visit to your headquarters and of its unhappy result,' said Holmes with some asperity. 'In view of that, I wonder why you have come to me. I had thought that I had made myself and my intentions perfectly clear.'

'And so you have, sir,' was the reply. 'I wish to persuade you to change your mind.'

'Indeed,' said Holmes with an intimidating lift of his eyebrows. 'And why should I deviate from my announced intention?'

'To save a life, Mr Holmes,' said the policeman, leaning forward.

'Say you so? Whose?' demanded Holmes, also leaning forward.

'A nameless drab,' replied Abberline. 'Some helpless unfortunate who, unless you help, Mr Holmes, will ply her trade one evening too often and end up as the next victim of the Whitechapel fiend.'

'Has there been some new development in the case?' asked Holmes eagerly.

'There has been no development of any kind,' returned the policeman. 'All has been quiet since the sending of the kidney some three weeks ago.'

'Then why do you seek my help now?'

'Because I know the Whitechapel area,' replied our visitor. 'Along with Superintendent Don Swanson, I am in charge of the hunt for Jack the Ripper. I have been in Whitechapel and Spitalfields constantly since we first realised that we had a lunatic on our hands. I have seen what is happening now happen before. I can read the signs, Mr Holmes, and I am afraid.'

'What signs do you read, Inspector?' asked Holmes.

'Well, sir, immediately following each murder the streets are as good as empty,' began Abberline. 'Only those who have the most pressing business dare venture out. For the women that those who do not understand their situation call the daughters of joy it is a simple choice between staying in at night and starving or going out on to the streets and risking death. Not a few are forced out. When nothing happens for a week or two people begin to hope that the fiend has had his day. Then life begins to return to normal – or as near to normal as it can ever be in the East End. That is the situation as it is at the moment, Mr Holmes. The time is ripe for another outrage. Indeed, I suspect that it will come within the next forty-eight hours.'

'How on earth could you possibly know that?' I cried.

'I do not know it, sir,' answered the policeman. 'I said that I suspected it.'

'And why do you suspect it?' asked Holmes

'Because during the next forty-eight hours the police in the Metropolis will have their hands full controlling the crowds that will flock to see the Lord Mayor's procession and will celebrate thereafter. If I were a murderer seeking a time to commit my crime, I could not ask for a better set of circumstances. The fear that followed the previous crimes has subsided and the police will be otherwise engaged. What more could a criminal want?'

'Only a victim,' said Holmes. 'And if my knowledge of the darker side of the life of our city is anything to go by, tonight every woman who ever walks a street will be out in her best, looking to see how much she can make from the revellers.'

'There you have it, Mr Holmes,' cried Abberline. 'Now you can see why I have come to you. I think that you are the only chance we have.'

'What do your superiors have to say to your line of reasoning?' asked Holmes.

'They have not the time to listen,' said the Inspector bitterly. 'They are too taken up with the details of routing the traffic so that His Worship will not be impeded.'

'Very well, then,' announced Holmes, 'if your own superiors are so little concerned over the fate of their reputations – to say nothing of the lives of those whom they are sworn to protect – I see no reason why I should alter my declared intention.'

'Mr Holmes, I understand your feelings, believe me,' said the Inspector. 'Is there nothing I can say to change your mind?'

'Nothing.'

'Perhaps if you will not listen to me,' said Abberline quietly, taking a foolscap envelope from his pocket, 'another might have more success. I was not to give this letter to you unless you refused absolutely your help.'

Holmes took the envelope impatiently and slit it open with his thumb. He unfolded and scanned the single page rapidly; his normally impenetrable features briefly registered surprise. He tossed the sheet to me and said with some sharpness, 'Where I had expected an apology and a supplication I find myself presented with a command.'

The letter bore an address in Whitehall, was dated with today's date and was not long.

Sherlock,
   It is imperative that you attend an interview with me
at my office immediately. Whatever case upon which
you are engaged must be abandoned at once. The Lady
who desires your assistance is more used to command
than to request and, although I am not at liberty to
mention her name in this communication, it might add
speed to your steps if I remind you that she still recalls
the service you did her son in the matter of a
photograph.
   The officer who presents this note to you has a four-
wheeler waiting. I expect you momentarily.
                                                          Mycroft

   I read the letter and was amazed as I realised the implications
of it. 'The Prince, the photograph. The Lady is –'
   '– in a great hurry, Watson, and have you not told me more
than once that it is impolite to keep a lady waiting?'
   True to the prediction in the letter, a four-wheeler awaited
us at the kerb and we were conveyed to Whitehall in a short
time. On the way I tried to arrive at an interpretation of the
recent turn of events that would even begin to make some sort
of sense, but it was beyond me. That the letter had come from
Holmes's brother, Mycroft, was obvious; though a bare two
months previously I would not have known that Holmes was
blessed with a brother, much less know his name and be able
to recognise his handwriting. I had made Mycroft Holmes's
acquaintance in the affair of the kidnapping and attempted
murder of Mr Paul Kratides of Athens and had learned from
Holmes that his brother supposedly occupied a lowly
appointment auditing the books of some obscure government
department but that his acuity of wit and his reasoning ability,
which surpassed even that of Holmes himself, caused him to
be consulted in matters of grave consequence, both political
and otherwise. What could have happened, I wondered, to
disturb Mr Mycroft Holmes and the Lady to whom he had
alluded?

Upon reaching our destination in Whitehall we discovered that word had been left at the desk that we were to be shown up the moment we arrived and so we were soon installed in Mycroft's room, the four of us making the office seem even smaller than it was.

Mycroft began the conversation without any preliminaries. 'That you are here, Sherlock,' he said, 'demonstrates that you have declined your assistance to Inspector Abberline. What reason have you for this obstinacy?'

Mycroft spoke sharply, his manner brusque and intimidating, but if he had hoped to overbear Holmes he was to be disappointed.

'What reason have you for urging me to greater pliancy?' he answered.

Mycroft made no reply but instead thanked Inspector Abberline for his assistance and bade him good morning. He walked back to his desk and sat down, motioning us to do the same. He placed his enormous hands upon his blotter and stared down at them for some moments. When, eventually, his great head came up and his eyes met his brother's he had the air of a man who has made up his mind.

'Sherlock, before I proceed I must ask you to give me your word that anything that you or Dr Watson may hear in this room, or anything that you may learn as a result, will be kept in the strictest confidence. For now and for ever.' His appearance was so grave and his manner so serious that, despite the implied insult to me, I could not take offence. Holmes noted my reaction and relaxed a little.

'As for myself, Mycroft,' he began, 'I will swear to nothing until I know more of the circumstances of the matter. I will give you my word that I will not by word or action or omission do anything that might bring harm to the country or to those of its citizens who are honest and law-abiding. As for my friend,' he went on, 'I will say only that he is the most decent man I have ever known.'

I felt an embarrassed glow at these words and told myself that Holmes had gone out of his way to say them simply to upbraid his brother for his rudeness. Mycroft appeared to have read no significance into them.

'Very well,' he said. 'His Lordship the Prime Minister has been instructed – note the word – by Her Majesty to ensure that you bring your powers to bear upon the matter of the Whitechapel murders. I have been deputised,' he smiled bleakly, 'for rather obvious reasons, to put the request to you.'

Holmes drew in a slow breath and twisted his hands in his lap. 'I cannot ignore an order from my Sovereign but, on the other hand, I have given my word –'

'– that you will not act until you have Warren's resignation as Commissioner of the Metropolitan Police,' said Mycroft. 'I have reason to believe that I will be able to put that document into your hand during the course of the day.'

'That would alter many things,' said Holmes.

'Warren informed Henry Matthews that he intends to submit his resignation today. It is something that he has done before and there is no reason why he should not do so now.'

'And this time the resignation will be accepted?' asked Holmes.

'The matter is in abeyance,' replied Mycroft, 'pending a decision upon a successor.'

'Jim Monro is the man,' said Holmes without hesitation.

'Her Majesty does not agree,' said his brother. 'She has, apparently, read Dr Watson's narrative of your investigation into the murder in Lauriston Gardens and has decided that you are the man for the job. She has instructed the Prime Minister to have the position offered to you.'

Holmes said nothing. I was about to offer my congratulations on an appointment that would show the world that his great talents had been recognised. But Holmes spoke before I did.

'Did Her Majesty also instruct that I should accept the post?'

Mycroft shook his head. 'She was most insistent that you should have a free choice.'

'In that case,' said Holmes, relieved, 'I decline.'

'Would you consider becoming the acting Commissioner, until such time as the Whitechapel murderer is caught?'

'If I am allowed a free choice here also,' said Holmes, 'then I will decline this offer as well. Are you now empowered to offer me the desk-sergeantship of the Bishopsgate Street police station?'

'No, my activities as an employment agency are at an end.' Mycroft paused thoughtfully and added, 'Or will be when I have secured the appointment of Monro for, as you, I believe him to be the man for the job. If Monro is appointed, will you work with him?'

'Only as far as I have to,' said Holmes. 'Monro is, or rather will be, like any other police officer, bound by the rules that regulate the discharge of police business; as long as I remain a private individual, I am not. In a conflict between the law and Justice my hands are not bound. It might be better for some of my plans if the police were not always aware of them.'

'But I need to be aware of them.' Mycroft stood and paced slowly and ponderously about the room. He stopped and faced us, the gravity of his expression even more pronounced than before. 'Warren's resignation will be accepted, without doubt,' he said. 'Once that happens the newspapers will be baying for Henry Matthews's blood and he may not be able to survive – he has neither competence nor popularity to keep him in his post – and if the Home Secretary falls . . . will Salisbury be safe?'

'The Prime Minister?' I asked, incredulous. 'Surely he would not be affected by the lack of confidence in the police force?'

'Not just the police force, Watson,' said Holmes. 'There are forces abroad in the country who would like nothing better than to hound the Government out of office; on whatever pretext. It was, you will recall, just a fortnight ago that we walked through the East End and spoke then of the disquiet and unrest spread by the anarchists and rabble-rousers, I think you called them.'

'But you surely cannot mean to suggest that such a crowd could hope to unseat a British Government?'

'Not on their own, perhaps,' said Mycroft, 'but when you add to the picture the Republicans, the Fenians, the Irish poor, who refer to Her Majesty as the "Famine Queen" and those self-seekers and charlatans who see their own route to advancement only over the ruins of the present system, there is, I think you will concede, cause for some concern. Sherlock, you must devise some means of bringing the Whitechapel murders to an end; and you must do it quickly. I am prepared to give you any help you may require that lies within my power. You and I are probably the two most devious men in London; we should be able to formulate some scheme that would serve. Have you any initial thoughts?'

'You are aware of Inspector Abberline's assessment of the situation in Whitechapel?' asked Holmes. 'Do you accept it?'

'I do,' replied Mycroft. 'That is why I suggested that he visit you. I had hoped to have you involved without my having to ask you. You know what government departments are,' he waved a massive hand in a dismissive gesture. 'I shall have to compile a report on this meeting, to be read by the Prime Minister himself. I had hoped to avoid this labour but now I shall have to follow the whole business through.'

'Don't, whatever you do, start a file,' warned Holmes with a chuckle, 'for if you do, it must have things put in it; it must be indexed, and logged; it must be regularly brought up to date; it must be copied, and checked, and audited. If you wish to maintain some degree of discretion, don't start a file.'

'I shan't, unless I am instructed so to do,' stated Mycroft. 'What do you propose to do now, Sherlock?'

'I shall go back to Baker Street, smoke a pipe or two and give the matter some thought. I shall communicate with you again when I have made some progress.'

With that we left the office and Holmes proved to be as good as his word. We returned with despatch to Baker Street and I waited, uncomplainingly, while Holmes smoked a briar of his vilest shag. He sat for some considerable time with his head sunk down upon his breast, gazing into the fire, and I had come to the conclusion that he had fallen asleep when he suddenly spoke.

'A change of perspective,' he said, 'that is what is required.'

He sprang up out of his chair and began to scribble upon a sheet of paper. When he had done he called for the boy and gave him the most detailed instructions as to how he was to deliver the note. Along with the directions Holmes also gave the promise of a couple of half-crowns upon the lad's return.

'You spoil that boy, Holmes,' I commented. 'I was under the impression that a shilling was his usual fee for delivering a message.'

'And so it is, usually,' agreed Holmes. 'But the increase in fee is due to the fact that the body for whom my message is intended could be almost anywhere in London. Young Billy will have earned his money if he can track down the elusive Wiggins.'

'You mean the foremost of your urchin confederates?' I asked.

'Just so,' replied Holmes. 'I rather think that I shall need their help tonight.'

More than that Holmes could not be drawn into saying. After a deal more thinking, and some pacing back and forth before the fire, he announced that he had to go out.

'Shall I accompany you?' I asked, beginning to rise.

'This time it will not be necessary for me to trouble you,' he said. 'In any event, I would like you to remain here so that you may pass this note to Wiggins should he call before I return.'

Having said this, Holmes paused only long enough to throw on his Inverness and to pick up his fore-and-aft and then was gone. Left to myself I began to put my papers, that had got into something of a disarray, what with our junket to France and all, into order. This proved to be a considerable undertaking and although the appearance of a cold buffet from Mrs Hudson indicated the passage of some hours I was amazed when Holmes finally reappeared to note that it was early evening already. As Holmes was hanging up his coat I told him that he had had no visitors during his absence.

'No, I know,' he said. 'Wiggins proved his efficacity by finding me. It was as well that he did, too, since, without him, I doubt that I should have made such a good haul.' As he said

66

this he unwrapped the bundle done up in brown paper that he had brought in with him. Whatever sense of smell I once had should have long since given up the ghost, what with Holmes's shag and chemicals, but it still functioned as I caught the reek of that bundle.

'In God's name, Holmes,' I cried, reaching for my bandanna, 'what have you brought back with you?'

'This is my costume for the evening,' he answered.

'You're surely not going to wear those?' I demanded. 'Quite apart from the fact that they contain more vermin than the laboratory at the London, they are women's clothes.'

'What else would one wear to disguise oneself as a woman?' asked my friend with that irritating superiority that he has when he knows that he is right – which is most of the time. 'Tonight I am to be a lady of the night.'

'Say rather a lady of the evening,' I said, 'for I doubt that you will live to see the night if you put those things on.'

'I shall keep my own linen next to my skin,' he said, 'and put my trust in carbolic.'

He now took out of the bundle a wig of fiery red hair, long and wavy, and a small bag of the type that the commoner women carried. His eyes lit upon the remains of my buffet and he fell upon them as though he had not eaten for a week. When he had consumed the last slice of tongue and the last crumb of bread he gathered up his pestiferous acquisitions and retired to his own room. He was in there for upwards of an hour and, had I not been watching the door the whole time and so known that he was the only person who could emerge from that room, I should not have known him when he reappeared.

You will have seen common prostitutes in the streets, of course. Not the elegant, laced and beribboned ladies that you see in the Haymarket or Piccadilly, but the drabs you have to avoid in Bishopsgate or Liverpool Street or any point east of there. Holmes had taken a foot off his height and used the women's clothes to such good effect that you could not detect the stoop. His face he had painted with that skill he has that would be the envy of many an actor. The powder on his forehead and around his eyes, that seemed to be there to hide the wrinkles, served only to emphasise them; the rouge upon his cheek only intensified the pallor of the rest of his face; the painted lips twitched into an ingratiating smile, only to show the rotting teeth they hid. All in all he was the epitome of the lowest form of unfortunate. Only one touch was missing.

'Your appearance is perfect,' I said, 'if such a description may be applied to such a picture, but you do not have about you that reek of gin that you and your sisters always have.'

'Gawd love yer, sir,' said the figure in a voice so unlike Holmes's that I looked again at the face, 'an' I'm just away to spend the shillin's Mr 'Olmes give me for makin' up 'is face.'

I laughed. 'You'll not catch me out as easily as that, Holmes. I have been watching the door ever since you entered your room. No one followed you. What do you say to that?'

'The lady preceded me into the room,' said the unmistakeable voice of Holmes. 'You did not notice because you were too busy being disgusted by the clothes I had bought.' The voice came, without a doubt, from Holmes's bedroom; so he must still be in there. The woman took a step towards me.

'Was you mentionin' somethin' about the odd drop o' gin, lovey?' she cooed. 'I'm in no 'urry. P'r'aps you an' me could get to know one anuvver a bi' better, like?' The salaciousness in her voice was sickening.

'Be off with you,' I roared, 'or you'll feel the weight of my cane across your shoulders.'

'And I had you marked down as a ladies' man, Watson,' said Holmes, flinging aside his bonnet and straightening up from his stoop. 'You disappoint me.'

'Were I to be faced by a lady,' I said stiffly, 'my reaction might have been different, though it has to be said that no lady would have gone unchaperoned into a gentleman's bed-chamber. How did you manage the voice? Are you about to take to the boards with a wooden dummy?'

'No,' he laughed. 'Though it was a performer in the halls who gave me the idea. It might prove useful to persuade some criminal that there was a Scotland Yarder behind him, might it not?'

'I confess that I can see no purpose in it,' I replied.

'Oh, I don't know, Doctor,' said Inspector Abberline from just behind me. I whirled about but there was no one there. I turned back to face Holmes and found myself staring down the barrel of his revolver. He gave a chuckle and said, 'You see, a knowledge of the theatrical is sometimes of use.'

'I had expected you to be wearing the red wig,' I said. 'It was only the fact that you were not that confounded me.'

'I need your help with the wig,' said Holmes. 'A man habitually wears so little hair that he is lost when faced with a superabundance of it. Come to my dressing-table and give me the benefit of your advice, if you would be so kind.'

It took only a few minutes to get the wig arranged to Holmes's satisfaction and securely pinned in place. Its effect was quite striking and not at all the sort of thing I would have expected an undercover agent to sport. I said as much to Holmes.

'I quite agree,' he said cheerfully. 'And I hope that anyone who might have cause to fear the spy will think the same. Now I must be going.'

'Do you wish me to accompany you?' I asked hopefully.

'I fear that we would not make a pair: you are too respectable by half, Watson.'

'Shall I shadow you, then?' I offered.

'That would not be a good idea,' said Holmes. 'A worthy doctor tracking a drab of my appearance through the back alleys of Whitechapel is likely to attract a considerable amount of the wrong sort of attention. Should you be fortunate enough to escape lynching at the hands of the mob the police are sure to be keen to interview you. In any case I have another task for you: one of the hardest that I could ask you to perform.'

'You have but to name it,' I said simply.

'Will you be my staging post, Watson? I have arranged with Wiggins that, if any news comes to Baker Street, he will see that I get it as soon as it may be carried across town. Wiggins, or one of his colleagues, will be in the kitchen all night. Give them any message you receive that you think I should have and they will see that it gets to me. By the same means if I should happen to pick up some reliable intelligence as to the identity of the fiend, I can send for my relief force. And if I do, I pray you come at your best speed and with a brace of pistols.'

'Have no fear upon that score,' I reassured him.

He said nothing but grasped my hand firmly for a moment and then was gone. After he had left I got out the Webleys and checked them both over carefully. I reamed them out, oiled them, wiped them clean and loaded them before laying them ready to hand on the table. This done, I changed into an old suit that would cause me no concern if it became involved in a scuffle. I tried then to interest myself in a yellow-back that I had started before we went to France but found, as I often did, that I could not concentrate on the feeble convolutions of the writer's imagination when my friend was out involving himself in some adventure more unbelievable than any author would dare to set before a reader. After pacing about for a while I sat down at my desk, filled the well and began to write up the notes that I had spent the afternoon sorting into order. But, like a compass drawn inexorably to one point, I kept wondering as to Holmes's progress – and his safety.

Although Watson did not know then, and indeed was never fully to know, what Holmes did that night, an account of his activities has been preserved. It was culled from his own note-book by Holmes himself. These notes are included here in their correct chronological place even though they were not prepared by Holmes until later for inclusion with his letter of the 5th of January 1889 which is reproduced in Chapter 13.

8.35 p.m. Into the street where Wiggins waited to guide me across the road and around the corner into York Terrace where Everson's van was parked. Entered the van and noted that Everson had not removed the hooks that had been fitted to facilitate the activities in Grosvenor Square.

8.55 p.m. Arrived at Everson's Commercial Road warehouse. Everson agreed to retain my normal street clothes so that they would be available without the necessity of visiting Baker Street should I need them in a hurry. (N.B. Everson says he will be at his store shifting furniture until breakfast time.) Consumed enough of the flask of gin that I had brought with me to taint my breath and allowed the remainder to soak into the front of my blouse to remedy the absence of the smell of liquor upon which Watson had commented.

9.45 p.m. The first opportunity I have had to make a note; though, in all truth, there has been little enough to note. I have spoken to innumerable people, none of whom has any solid data as to the murders but each of whom has a theory to propound. Have made my way from the Commercial Road by way of Philpot Street and Mount Street; thence across the Whitechapel Road. Writing this under a light in a court off Brady Street. Plan to move westwards towards Spitalfields Market where I should be able to rest again. Taking a foot off my height is hard on my legs.

11.05 p.m. Junction of Lamb Street and Crispin Street, writing by the light of a small lamp: covering the action by appearing to charge a cracked clay I have acquired. If my efforts continue to yield such small results, the pipe is likely to be the most valuable thing I will secure tonight. Will move on down Crispin Street and, via Wentworth Street, into Thrawl Street and Flower & Dean Street: surely the vilest streets in London.

11.45 p.m. *Tempus omnia revelat.* Not so much a shaft as a glimmer of light. It was in the Britannia, or the Ringer's as it is known locally from the name of the woman who runs it, that I saw her. When I entered the place I automatically subjected the crowd of loafers and petty thieves inside to a careful scrutiny. And I happened upon a countenance with which I was familiar. A young, square-faced woman. A lull in the general level of noise in the place enabled me to hear her voice and as soon as I caught the lilt in her speech, I had her. She was Mary

71

Jane, who had been Watson's slavey for a short period during the time he had deserted Baker Street to set up his own establishment with his beloved Constance. The drop in the level of sound enabled me to hear her announce that she was going out to earn herself 'a few coppers'. I was only three paces behind her by the time she reached the street.

She walked down to White Street and along that almost to Middlesex Street before my increasingly stentorian wheezing attracted her befuddled attention. The conversation that followed lacked the social niceties but was germane to the matter in hand; and at the end of it I felt, for the first time, that I might, at last, be able to achieve something.

Mary Jane, of course, did not know me but I convinced her that I am one of the regular patients at Watson's clinic at the London. I told her that Watson was asking for information – in the strictest confidence – relating to the murders because I have been asked to look into them. Watson, I'd said, was offering ten pounds for any worthwhile data and his police crony, Sherlock 'Olmes, was willing to give twice that for first-rate information. I received the distinct impression that for the chance of earning thirty pounds she would do practically anything. I also gathered from her unguarded comments that she was somewhat behind with the rent – she wondered why she had not already been thrown out of her room – and that she believed herself to be pregnant. She mused briefly of not claiming a monetary reward from Watson but of taking her fee in his services instead.

Agreed to meet again at about seven-thirty in the morning at her room at Number 13, Miller's Court; just off Dorset Street. Opposite Crossingham's.

The next three and a half pages of Holmes's notes show him criss-crossing Whitechapel and Spitalfields for the remainder of the night asking questions when he could and eavesdropping whenever he heard anybody talking of the murders. Dawn found him in the pubs around Spitalfields Market, which opened early to cater for the market staff and customers, where he decided to have breakfast and

*rest his legs – which must have been killing him since, as he says,
he'd been taking a foot off his height for a period of several hours.
Eventually it was time for him to make his way to Dorset Street.*

7.25 a.m. Made my way to Miller's Court which was situate
midway along the northern side of Dorset Street. This
thoroughfare was darker by daylight than it had been during
the hours of darkness, owing to the fact that the lodging-
houses' lights had been extinguished. The court's entrance was
by way of a narrow passage – barely a yard wide – fronted by
an opening the size of a guardsman's sentry box and passing
between a common lodging-house and, on the left-hand side,
a chandler's shop.

The court itself was small; no more than thirty feet long by
ten wide. There were three houses upon either side of the court
and, surprisingly, those houses had been whitewashed up to the
level of the first-floor windows.

Having knocked at Number 13 twice and elicited no
response, I moved to the window which I had noticed had a
broken pane and drew aside the faded muslin curtain and the
old coat that had been hung inside it. The sight that met my
gaze was such that I pushed up the sash of the window at once
and climbed in; so that I might not be observed in the court.

On a bedstead that had been pushed against the other side
of the room lay what was left of Mary Jane Kelly. She had been
killed, mutilated almost beyond recognition and left on the bed
as though she were an interesting anatomical specimen for
discussion by a group of medical students. I must set down,
while the image remains in my remembrance, the observations
that I made.

The skin of the face had been removed, laying bare the whole
of the frontal bone, the malars and the superior and inferior
maxillaries. Both the ears and the nose had been removed. The
throat had been slashed across – and this was the cause of death.
The splashes of arterial blood upon the wall clearly showed that
her heart had still been beating when the knife had been drawn
across her throat. The chest and abdomen resembled nothing

so much as a rib or saddle of lamb after it had been stripped at the cold table.

The flesh of the thorax had been stripped away so that the ribs showed through. The pectoral muscles had been ignored; some of the flesh had been removed from the arms and the thighs had been skinned but this had been done in a hurried and desultory manner as though the murderer had reserved his attention for other areas. The internal organs of the abdomen, for example.

Such of the internal organs as were still identifiable could be located in various positions in the room. The liver had been left upon the bed between the feet of the victim; the gall-bladder, pancreas, duodenum and suprarenal capsules had all been mangled and pushed into the space in the right hypochondriac and epigastric regions that had remained upon the removal of the liver. The right kidney was upon the floor beneath the bed. The part of the bladder not remaining in the body had been tossed against the wall. Nor had this random distribution of dismembered flesh been confined to the bed and floor. The skin and flesh stripped from the lower limbs, together with the nose and breasts, had been placed upon the table beside the bed.

The room in which this shambles had occurred revealed no particulars of singular interest: it was about twelve feet square and contained, apart from the bedstead, only two tables and a chair. On the chair were piled the clothes that the victim had been wearing when I had spoken to her earlier. (N.B. If M.J.K. had undressed and taken her killer to bed with her it was likely that he, too, had disrobed. Obviously, therefore, there would be no bloodstains on his clothes. Equally obviously, this comment would not apply to the previous slayings, which had occurred outdoors.)

In the grate were the remains of an intense fire whose constituents had comprised various items of women's clothing including the remnants of a straw bonnet. There were also the remains of a kettle. That the fire had been a fierce one was proved by the fact that the kettle's spout had melted. The murderer undoubtedly used the kettle to boil water so that, having avoided bloodstains on his clothes, he was able to wash off the blood he could not have avoided upon his person. Considering the way in which the victim had been dismembered, he must have been red to the elbows, at the very least.

10.00 a.m. Everson has provided a mug of tea, after reluctantly accepting that I did not wish to share his breakfast, and I drink as I write. I must take care to set down what has occurred exactly as it happened. After my examination of Mary Kelly I turned my bull's-eye round so as to extinguish it and, by its light, saw that the front of the blouse I was wearing had become bloodstained. I knew that I could not walk through the streets in such a condition. I had no fears for my safety but I at once foresaw that I would be noticed and when the news of the murder became public I would be remembered. Inevitably the bloodstained lady would lead the police a long way away from the real perpetrator of the crime and I was loath to mislead a force that was going to be confused enough. I took the shawl that Mary Jane had been wearing the night before from the bottom of the pile on the chair and threw it around my shoulders, arranging it so that it hid the stains.

I climbed out through the window and walked quickly down the passage and out into Dorset Street. As I stepped out of the passage I practically collided with a woman on the pavement. She turned to me and asked, 'What brings you up so early, Mary?' I saw at once that my appropriation of the dead woman's shawl together with the fact that I had chosen a wig that was the same colour as Mary Kelly's hair had convinced this person that I was Mary Kelly. I stumbled against the wall, using the movement to huddle the shawl closer about me and consider what I could say in answer to the question. I slurred my speech and tried out an accent: 'I have the horrors of drink upon me.' 'Why don't you go into Mrs Ringer's and have half a pint of beer?' asked my solicitous friend. A small pile of vomit in the gutter provided the answer this time: 'I have been there and had it,' I said, 'but I have brought it all up again.' My companion followed my gaze to the gutter, said something about pitying my feelings and having to get her husband's breakfast and departed towards Bishopsgate Street. I made my best speed back to Commercial Road where a wash, shave and change back into my own clothes, followed by a cup of tea and bread and dripping have put me into the frame of mind to write these last notes while the events are still quite clear in my mind.

I am, of course, in a very delicate position. Upon the one hand, I have informed the Metropolitan force, within whose jurisdiction Mary Jane had been done to death, that I will have no more to do with the case, yet, upon the other, I have stumbled upon the body and have had the opportunity to examine it in some detail. Is it not clearly my duty to report the outrage? How Sir Charles Warren will relish that! Now that he can no longer instantly have me clapped into irons on some trumped-up charge he will certainly spread the story that my amateur bumblings have so disturbed the scene of the crime that the official investigation has been irreparably harmed. Modesty does not blind me to the fact that my name and reputation are such that the argument over the damage or otherwise that I might have caused would rapidly obscure the original issue: that of discovering the murderer. I will keep my knowledge to myself; at least for the time being.

10.35 a.m. I arrived back at Baker Street. I found the good doctor asleep in his chair beside the fire with a loaded pistol in his lap and I saw that there was another lying on the table. He awakened as I entered and insisted that I give him an account of the night's adventures. I gave him a narrative that left out a great deal but I did mention, casually, that I had seen his old slavey, Mary Jane. He was not surprised, saying that his wife had always said she would end her days in the slums. Watson retired to his room to wash, shave and dress and I rang for breakfast for him and coffee for both of us. I began the newspapers and, when Watson returned, we soon fell into the settled routine. I found it difficult, however, to concentrate upon the papers when every moment I expected the ring on the bell that would announce that the body had been found.

Noon Still no news. I have read the newspapers twice, the second time even reading the details of the preparations that had been made for the Lord Mayor's procession: dull reading indeed.

4.00 p.m. The news at last. There came a great ringing of our door bell, followed by raised voices when our landlady opened the door and a pounding upon the stairs as somebody came up them two or three at a time. The door was almost kicked open and Inspector Abberline rushed into the room. 'The fiend has struck again, Mr Holmes, in Miller's Court, off Dorset Street. Will you come and examine the scene?' I said that I would and Watson and I retired to don coat and boots. As I emerged from my room there came a new knock at the door and within a few seconds a young constable was ushered into the room. He began to speak quietly to the inspector but looked up as Watson came out of his room. The constable's jaw dropped and he reached for his truncheon, saying as he did so, 'Why, sir, that's him. That's Jack the Ripper!'

CHAPTER 6

Suspicions

From now on we may return to Watson's own narrative, at least for the present.

I have been in some tight places in my time but I have never felt at so complete a loss as when the young constable pointed his finger at me and cried: 'Sir, that's the man: that's Jack the Ripper!'

Inspector Abberline stood looking almost as bemused as I was, but he recovered a little more quickly. He turned upon the constable as would a wife who found her husband in dalliance with another woman; and than that there is no greater rage.

'I am aware that the situation is grim indeed,' said Abberline tightly, 'and that any attempt to bolster up flagging spirits is to be commended, but I find your humour somewhat misplaced. Do you know who these gentlemen are?'

'I have no idea who this gentleman is,' answered the constable, indicating Holmes, 'but I have every reason to believe that this gentleman,' indicating me, 'is the Whitechapel murderer. I took him into custody some time ago, but he was released upon the order of some inspectors at the station to which I took him.'

Abberline looked as though somebody had hit him on the head with a heavy weight, I stood spluttering helplessly, but Holmes was equal to the situation.

'When did this incident occur?' he asked sharply.

'Well, I can't be sure without checking my note-book,' said the young policeman, 'but it was about the middle of August, that I do remember.'

'As I recall we were not very busy at that time,' said Holmes musingly. 'What do you say to these charges, Watson?'

'Why, Holmes,' I said, 'what do you expect me to say to them? I deny them utterly.'

'A not altogether unexpected occurrence,' commented Holmes drily. He turned to the constable and was about to ask him some more questions when he caught sight of the expression on his face. 'What's the matter, constable? Are you ill?'

For answer the young man sprang across the room and seized my left hand which he dragged round into the light of the nearest lamp. After he had spent several seconds closely inspecting my hand he let it drop and turned away saying, 'It isn't there. It isn't there.'

'What isn't there?' demanded Abberline, who had now recovered from his initial surprise. 'What are you talking about?'

The young constable now looked rather crestfallen but set his shoulders and began to explain. 'Well, sir, it was after the first two murders,' he began, 'when we were first told to be on our toes. I had the idea of working my beat backwards, so as to fox anybody who knew the times of the beats, and I came across an unfortunate I know called Rosy sitting on a brick dustbin in Henage Court talking to a well-dressed gentleman who was the living image of this gentleman here, sir, except that he had a scar on the palm of his left hand, which this gentleman doesn't. Apart from that I would have sworn that this was the man. Anyway I thought he was worth taking back to the station, so I asked him to come along with me, which he did.

'When we got back to the station there were a number of inspectors there and I thought I was going to be commended for my sharpness in bringing in a suspect but all they did was ask him who he was and when he said that he was a doctor from Brixton, they let him go. They didn't ask him what a doctor from Brixton was doing in a dark court at that hour of the morning with a common drab. I should've liked to have heard his answer to that question.'

'What was his name?' asked Holmes.

'He didn't say his name, sir,' replied the constable, 'he merely produced his card and the inspectors read it. They didn't even ask him to open the bag he was carrying.'

'Did he at any time during your journey from Henage Court make any attempt to escape?' asked my companion.

'No, sir, he did not.'

'Do you not find that most suggestive?' asked Holmes.

'In what way?' countered the constable.

'Isn't it obvious?' snapped Abberline. 'If you were the most wanted man in London, arrested by a single constable and with a bag full of razors and knives, wouldn't you attempt an escape? Even if it meant attacking the policeman? I'm sure that I would.'

'And so, I suspect, would most guilty men,' added Holmes. 'You say this man bore a resemblance to Watson here?'

'Very much so,' said the young man. 'Perhaps if you saw them side by side you would perceive differences but apart they look very alike.' He turned to me and said, 'I'm sorry, sir, for any upset that I might have caused you. But, just for the moment there, I thought you were that man again.'

'And yet it is getting on for three months since you last saw that man,' said Holmes. 'How could you be so certain?'

'I have been transferred since then, sir, and my beat now takes in Liverpool Street. I have seen him there several times since the night I arrested him. I always say to him, "Hello, Jack, still after the ladies?" whereupon he runs away as fast as he can go.'

'Interesting,' said Holmes.

'You think so?' asked Inspector Abberline. 'I rather think that this young man has allowed his imagination to run away with him. I have always held that too much imagination is bad for a policeman.'

'It is that spirit that makes the Metropolitan Police force what it is today,' said Holmes.

'Why, thank you sir,' said Abberline. 'It is comforting to know that our efforts are appreciated.'

Holmes had apparently lost interest. He had gone to the mantel and begun to fill a pipe. He said nothing further until he had filled it to his satisfaction and got it safely alight. Then he turned back to Abberline and said, 'All this has rather taken us away from the original purpose of your visit, Inspector. I believe you wanted us to take a look at the scene in – where was it? Miller's Court? – before any clue that might be there to find had been obscured.'

'That's what I came to say, sir,' said the young policeman. 'The body has been removed and any number of people have been into the room since you left. I don't think that even Mr Holmes could make very much of what is left, sir.'

'Damn their eyes!' cried Abberline. 'Our first chance to let Mr Holmes view a body as it was found gone.'

'I should not be too chagrined if I were you,' said Holmes. 'I am sure that a killer of the sort that we are up against here would not leave any clue to his identity behind him.'

'You are right, Mr Holmes,' replied the Inspector. 'I went over that room myself and will pit my reputation that there was nothing in there that would lead any man to the murderer. But I thought it best to ask you to have a look, Mr Holmes. You have solved seemingly impossible problems before.'

'I am glad that I have your confidence at any rate,' said Holmes. 'Tell me, what did you find out before you came here? You were at the scene of the crime and you most certainly would have asked for witnesses.'

'Indeed I did, Mr Holmes,' said the Inspector warmly. 'And I found any number of them.'

'Do you say so?' said Holmes, putting another match to his pipe, which had, in fact, not caught with the first one. 'And what did your witnesses have to say for themselves? More swarthy foreigners with staring eyes and bloody collars, I'll be bound.'

'For all the information they can give,' said Abberline slowly, 'they may as well be blind and deaf, since they saw and heard nothing. Except for one who claims to have witnessed an event more remarkable than any in my experience.'

'You don't mean that the murderer was seen at his evil work?' I asked, amazed that so cunning a killer could have made so elementary a mistake.

'Nothing so commonplace. This witness, a woman named Maxwell, claims to have seen, and spoken to, the victim at half-past eight this morning.'

'But, why is that in any way remarkable?' I asked, puzzled.

'Because the doctor said that he was sure that the woman had been dead for several hours when she was found at about eleven o'clock. He won't be sure until he's carried out a more thorough investigation but he thinks the murder took place some time between midnight and four o'clock. So, it would be unusual for the victim to be talking to Mrs Maxwell four and a half hours after she had been killed, would it not?'

'If the doctor is right,' I said, 'this Maxwell woman must either be drunk or lying. She could hardly be mistaken about something that took place so short a time ago.'

'That is the only good thing about her evidence. We'll see if we can get her to remember any details, but I'm not very sort of woman. More respectable than I would have looked to finding in Dorset Street.'

'Do you have any other statements that are of interest?' asked Holmes.

'I'm afraid not, Mr Holmes,' said Abberline. 'As I said, the others are basically from people who didn't see anything; except for a laundress who claimed to have seen a man standing about in Dorset Street between two and three in the morning.'

'What description did she give?' asked Holmes eagerly.

'None, I'm afraid,' said the Inspector. 'She said that she saw a man but that she couldn't describe him.'

'At least she wasn't claiming to have seen a walking corpse,' I remarked.

'That is the only good thing about her evidence. We'll see if we can get her to remember any details, but I'm not very hopeful.' Abberline certainly did not sound hopeful.

Holmes tried to encourage him as he shepherded the two policemen out of the room, but I fear he did not succeed. When we were alone Holmes sat down by the fire and stared into the flames as if trying to read the answers to all his questions in the blaze. Knowing his mood and knowing that he would not wish to be disturbed until he had had the time to collect his thoughts I seated myself at my desk and sought to concentrate upon some outstanding correspondence.

After almost an hour had passed in silence Holmes gave a snort and levered himself to his feet. He recharged his pipe and began to pace about the floor. I knew the signs; he had come to a decision and was reviewing it prior to setting it out for me. I put the writing things away and waited for him to speak. When he did the words were slow-paced and addressed more to himself than to me.

'We are still approaching this problem from the wrong direction,' he announced. 'I do not believe that we will ever be fortunate enough to catch our man in the act, nor do I consider it likely that he will oblige the police by making himself obvious enough for them to notice him. So, if he will not come to us we will have to flush him out of hiding.'

'You think that he is in hiding then?' I queried.

'Not literally, perhaps,' said Holmes, 'but it is a fact that he is not exactly advertising his whereabouts. You will recall, Watson, the way a hunter would draw out a man-eater that had been terrorising a native village in the sub-continent.'

'A Judas goat!' I exclaimed.

'Exactly,' said Holmes. 'But where to find one, that's the question.'

'I'm sure I have no idea,' I said sadly.

'But I am sure that you have,' replied Holmes with that infernal smile in his eye again.

'What on earth do you mean?' I asked.

'Do you not attend a clinic in the heart of the Whitechapel district?' asked Holmes eagerly. 'Do you not meet and talk with women of the same class as the victims every week?'

'You know that I do,' I confessed, bewildered. I could not see where this line was leading.

'Could not a man of your acuteness and with your insight into

83

the female mind find a woman who would be prepared to help us bring the miscreant to justice? For the benefit of her sisters of the pavement – and her purse.'

'For the latter rather than the former, I fear,' I said. 'But could you not recreate your character of last night to trap the fiend?'

'I fear not,' replied Holmes. 'We will need a separate lure so that the two of us will be available to man the guns. We are dealing with a ruthless and very clever man who will not be trapped easily. He will see through a deception unless we are most thorough. You will have to select a woman of courage and intelligence, Watson, and we will have to devise a plot that will take in our Jack.'

Holmes retreated to his armchair and I knew that I would not hear another word from him for a considerable period so I fell to a contemplation of the women I treated at the clinic. There were few that I would consider had the mental ability to carry out any but the simplest tasks. I wondered if Holmes knew what he was asking when he suggested that I find a patient who would, and could, act as our bait. The women who came to the clinic were, as often as not, the very worst of those you see on the streets. Ill-educated, unhealthy drabs, old before their time – and looking even older – they were not the type of woman popularised by the writers of pamphlets dealing with the histories of unfortunate young ladies who, usually through no fault of their own, became "daughters of joy". My patients were more the sort of women you would have looked to see clustered at the foot of a busy guillotine during the height of the Terror.

I let my eyes roam about the room as I racked my mind for a solution to the problem that Holmes had set me: almost as if I expected something that I looked at to suggest an answer to me. I smiled to myself at the thought, knowing that there was no . . .

Unless . . . Yes, perhaps there was a possibility. One particular woman whose only problem was an over-indulgence in gin. If she could be persuaded to put her inclination aside for a few days she might well answer our needs.

'Holmes—' I began, but he did not allow me to finish.

'Who is she, Watson?' He saw my confusion and laughed a little. 'Your face is as easy to read as a broadsheet poster. I can see that you have thought of a woman who might serve our purpose, have you not?'

'I am surprised that you cannot read her name, age, and affliction in my countenance as easily as you read everything else,' I said rather stiffly. No man likes to be told that he may be sifted at a glance.

'Her name is Amelia, she is of middle years and her weakness is an addiction to hard liquor, nothing more.'

'By all that is wonderful, Holmes!' I cried in genuine amazement, 'how on earth could you possibly know that?'

'By using my eyes, my memory and my knowledge of your intelligence and integrity,' replied Holmes smoothly. ' First, my eyes. You sat with a deep frown of concentration upon your face until your glance happened upon the print that you have had framed as a birthday gift for one of your colleagues at the hospital.'

'But it is wrapped in waxed paper and bound with cord,' I protested.

'Yes, but you told me, when you brought it home the other day, that it was a representation of the gallant action of the sloop *Amelia* against a French two-decker that was attempting to run the Brest blockade in '05. So, the name Amelia had fired your interest. Now, I had asked you to consider your patients and so it is a safe bet that this Amelia is one of that number and since you have told me a number of times that you deal with that group of unfortunates that is no longer in the first flush of youth but which is not yet so aged as to be unable to walk the streets her age is surely no mystery. As to her weakness, that is a simple matter. You would not suggest a woman who was too infirm to be of use but you would suggest one whom you thought would forgo the pleasures of the bottle for a week or so if the reward were attractive enough. Am I not right?'

'You are right on every count, of course,' I said, wondering why something that seemed so obvious now had seemed so very marvellous just a few seconds beforehand. 'But I must decline to give you her name for the time being. With such risk involved as will inevitably attend this enterprise, I must first sound the lady to test her inclination. You will agree with that, I hope.'

'My dear Watson,' said Holmes warmly, 'I would insist upon it. Firstly because it would do your reputation little good to have a patient misled or tricked into a dangerous situation which she did not fully comprehend and secondly because I would not wish to set a trap with a bait that was not reliable. When do you think that you will be able to speak to this woman?'

'If we are in luck she may be at the clinic tonight,' I said. 'I will tackle her then.'

'Let us hope that we have a little luck this evening,' said Holmes. 'It is about time that fortune favoured us rather than our adversary.'

CHAPTER 7

The Judas Goat

In the event, Dr Watson's hope that the woman he wanted to sound out would be at the clinic 'tonight' – that is, the 9th of November – was rather optimistic. His diary records that it was not until almost a week had gone by that he had the opportunity of testing her reaction to Holmes's idea. These extracts from Watson's diary recommence with his description of the events of the evening of the 15th of November 1888.

It was with considerable trepidation that I approached the portals of the London for the fourth consecutive evening and the sixth during the last week. I had begun to fear that some catastrophe had befallen the woman whom I had thought of as being suitable for our purposes and that I should have to think of another. This I had tried to do – and had failed. I could bring to mind nobody with the keenness of wit required for the job. I had carefully watched all the women I had been called upon to treat but had seen none who seemed to be in any way suitable. I had asked all and sundry to tell my first choice that I wished to see her and had asked after her so assiduously that I was now having to bear the chafes and japes of my younger colleagues and the disapproving glances of my seniors. At first I had not known whether I should be amused or enraged by these reactions but in the end I decided that I would be best advised to ignore them. I knew what I was doing and I knew why I was doing it. Let the others think what they might; I would have the last laugh.

The porter returned my hail cheerfully as I came up with his lodge but shook his head as I began to ask my nightly question.

'No, sir,' he called, 'I ain't seen 'ide nor 'air of 'er.'

I received this news as resignedly as I could and made my way towards the area reserved for the out-patients clinic. I cast my eye over the people who were waiting for the clinic to begin but could see no sign of the woman I sought. I felt a little depressed. Providing the right bait had seemed one of the few ways in which I could actively help Holmes in what could well turn out to be one of his most important and famous cases and I was unable to keep up my part. Although Holmes had said nothing to me I knew that he chafed at the delay and had been giving thought to alternative stratagems to be employed in the event that a suitable lure could not be found. I had seen him once or twice finger the red wig he had worn the night he had been out searching for information as though he were considering how his impersonation of the type of woman our adversary was likely to pick for his next victim could be put to a more effective use.

Seated behind the desk in the tiny, curtained-off alcove that gave the illusion of privacy to those who sat in the chair opposite, I rang the bell to indicate that I was ready to receive the first patient. Hardly had the sound of the bell died away when the orderly twitched the curtain aside.

'Beg pardon, Doctor,' he began, 'but that – er – lady you've been asking after is outside.'

'Is she, by Jove?' I cried standing up and reaching for my coat.

'Shall I show her in?' he asked dubiously.

'No,' I said. 'I'll see her outside. You go and find a cab. Bring it to the main entrance and have it wait. I'll be there directly. Oh, and you'd better ask one of the other doctors to see my patients this evening; I doubt that I will be able to return tonight.'

He looked a little startled at my instructions but hurried off to do as he was bid. I struggled into my coat – which is always a bother because of my shoulder – threw all my implements back into my bag and clapped on my hat. Then I strode out of the alcove and looked about until I spotted her. She was standing by one of the doors to the corridor and she was not paying any attention to what was going on inside the waiting area. I walked over to her without her being aware that I was in the room.

'Good evening, Amelia,' I said. 'How are we tonight?'

'Well, I don't know about you,' she snapped, 'but I wouldn't be here if I was all right, would I?'

'And I thought it was me that you came to see,' I said with a smile. I think it was the smile that softened her. Holmes always says that my smile would have been enough to melt even Mrs Brownrigg's heart and Constance used to say that my smile over the fresh linen of the breakfast table was like the sun shining upon a snow-covered landscape. Whatever the truth of it was, Amelia immediately blushed and began to stammer an apology. I cut her short.

'I want you to come with me,' I told her, 'to see a friend of mine.'

'But I want you to give me something for my chest,' she said.

'The only things your chest needs,' I said severely, 'are some warm clothes on the outside and a little less spirit on the inside. And I think I might have found a way to see that you get both of those things. Come along, I've got a cab waiting.'

'What?' she said. 'A hansom?'

'The most effective way of finding out is to cut along,' I pointed out. She needed no second urging and set out for the door at a lick that many a woman half her years might have envied. We went outside and piled into the waiting cab in short order and it was not long before we heaved ourselves out into Baker Street. We had spoken not a word during our journey and I had watched my fellow passenger's face during the trip. When the initial novelty of riding instead of walking had worn off I could see the second thoughts as they formed in her mind. Indeed, one did not need to possess the gifts of my fellow lodger to know what was passing through her mind. It had not yet been a week since the last of the Whitechapel murderer's outrages and the newspapers had been filled since then with speculation that the killer was in possession of considerable medical knowledge and had affiliated surgical skill. None had, so far as I knew, gone so far as to say that only a doctor could be responsible for the atrocities but the inference had been there for any who wished to take it up.

So it was that, as the cab clattered away and left the two of us alone upon the pavement, I could see the fear and uncertainty in my patient's eyes. I hope I may not be thought immodest or unwarrantably full of swagger if I say that I believe the woman beside me trusted and respected me, but at the same time, I knew, her whole training and experience had taught her that men are not to be trusted. And, I dare say, the men with whom she usually consorted were not. I attempted to put her mind at ease concerning her present position. Instead of using my key I tugged on the bell wire. After a few moments Billy answered the door and I brought our visitor into the hallway.

'Billy, be so kind as to announce us,' I said. 'Dr Watson and his patient. Tell Mr Sherlock Holmes that I have brought the lady of whom I told him. Then ask Mrs Hudson to send up some coffee.'

Billy blinked once, collected himself and sped off upon his errands. We followed him up the stairs and entered into the sitting-room. Holmes was standing by the mantel with a pipe in his hand and he obviously realised what I was attempting to do by having us announced since he came forward with his free hand extended and said, 'My dear Dr Watson, how pleasant to see you again. And who is your companion?'

I risked a sideways glance at her and saw that she was responding in just the way I had hoped. I had feared that she would be suspicious of my motives in bringing her to the house and so I had sought to reassure her that there was no cause for unease. I had succeeded better than I had hoped to in that I had underestimated the power of Holmes's reputation. As soon as my eyes lit upon her face I realised that she would cooperate with whatever scheme my friend had in mind. I recollected myself and made the introductions.

'Amelia, may I present Mr Sherlock Holmes, whom I am privileged to call a friend. Holmes, this is Mrs Amelia Palmer.'

I stopped as a thought struck me and I turned to the woman I had brought into the room and asked, 'Or is it Farmer? I've never been quite sure. Both names appear in the hospital records.'

'I've never been sure myself,' she answered, 'but that's no wonder considerin' my husband never knew 'imself.'

'It is of no consequence, in any event,' said Holmes coming forward and taking her hand. 'Please come and sit down by the fire. You must be cold after your journey.'

'Oh no,' said Amelia, 'we came 'ere in a hansom so I didn't 'ave time to catch cold.'

Holmes smiled, said he was pleased to hear it and suggested that she should sit in his velvet armchair. I sat myself in my usual seat opposite and Holmes drew up the cane-backed chair for himself. He did not sit in it, however, since there was a knock at the door and he went to answer it. He came with a tray upon which our landlady had put a pot of coffee along with milk, sugar, cups and saucers. He put the tray upon the dinner table and served us all before he sat down himself.

'Has the good Doctor given you any indication of what I wanted to talk to you about?' asked Holmes when he had settled himself into his chair.

'No. He only said you would like to see me.'

'I thought that it would sound better coming from you,' I said. I did not point out that since Holmes had not seen fit to enlighten me as to his plans it would have been little short of miraculous had I been able to explain them to our visitor.

Holmes came directly to the point. 'Tell me, Mrs Palmer, how much do you earn in a week?'

Amelia was a little disturbed by the question but she pulled herself together and answered, 'I work at trousers finishing and I can make almost seven shillings in a good week; if the material is easy to work. If it's a tough material to work, then I probably make about five shillings. Why do you want to know?'

'Because I want to give you the chance to earn more money in a couple of weeks than you have earned during the rest of the year,' replied my friend. Amelia looked at me and I smiled to reassure her that all was well. She looked a little disappointed, I thought. She turned back as Holmes began to speak again. 'I would like you to perform a service for me. I suppose you would not call it pleasant but it is certainly not arduous.'

'What sort of a service?' she asked and then gave Holmes no time to answer. She stood up and said, 'Don't bother to tell me, I don't want to know.' She turned to me and asked bitterly, 'And where will you be, Doctor, while I am performing this service for your fine friend?'

The question took me unawares. 'I – I'm afraid I have no idea.'

'He will be at the back,' said Holmes absently, 'while I cover the front. I have given the matter great thought and I consider that to be the most satisfactory arrangement.'

Amelia's eyes had gone wide at Holmes's words and she stood staring down at him as though she did not believe that she had heard him correctly. She shook herself like a pug awakening from an afternoon doze and put down her coffee cup. She drew herself up to her full height and said coldly, 'I thank you for the coffee, sir, and will take my leave of you now.'

'You mean you're leaving?' I asked. The question reads rather stupidly but I could not believe that she was going to turn down Holmes's offer without even knowing what was involved. 'Don't you want to know what you will have to do to earn the money?'

'No, sir, I don't,' she replied firmly. 'I know that I am poor and that I have led a life that can't be called blameless but I've never considered doing anythin' of the kind you're suggestin'. I would rather starve first.'

Holmes looked completely at a loss, which is a rare state indeed for him, and seemed unable to think of anything to say when I suddenly realised what had happened. 'Holmes,' I said, 'I rather think that Mrs Palmer has misunderstood the nature of the service of which you are talking.'

Comprehension flooded into my friend's face as he realised what I meant. He sprang out of his chair with such vigour that Amelia took a step backwards.

92

'My dear Mrs Palmer,' began Holmes in his most disarming voice, 'please accept my humblest apologies if anything that I have said has caused you to think that I was trying to – er – how shall I put it –?'

'You mean to say that you weren't tryin' to proposition me?' asked our visitor suspiciously.

'Yes, I have a proposition for you,' said Holmes, 'but it is not of a – er – carnal nature. Let me reassure you upon that score.'

Amelia did not look very reassured, though whether this was because she did not trust Holmes or whether she did not understand what he was saying, I could not be sure. Holmes seemed to realise this as well and said, 'If you would take your seat again for a few moments I will try to explain what I mean.'

Amelia took her seat again and accepted the refilled coffee cup that I offered her. Holmes lit his pipe and began to fill the room with the odour of his tobacco, which, I was delighted to note, was considerably more pleasant than usual. After a few minutes' silence he began to speak.

'Firstly, Mrs Palmer,' he said, 'I want you to understand that there is an element of danger in what I want you to do. Both Dr Watson and myself will be on hand at the moment when this danger occurs and will do all in our power to minimise the risks, but,' Holmes paused to allow his words to take effect, 'we cannot guarantee your safety.'

'This service is somethin' to do with your police work then?' asked our guest.

'Yes, it is,' replied Holmes. 'I want you to act as the bait in a trap designed to catch a desperate criminal. Will you do it?'

There was a short pause in the conversation and then Amelia asked, 'Who is this criminal?'

'The Whitechapel murderer,' said Holmes simply.

'What? Jack the Ripper?' breathed our visitor.

Holmes merely nodded. I had expected then a blanket refusal but, instead, there was another pause. Eventually Amelia asked, 'How much are you going to pay me if I say I'll do it?'

'I will pay you one hundred pounds whether we succeed in

catching the man or not,' said Holmes, and after waiting a few seconds for this figure to register in her mind he added a further inducement. 'And, if the murderer is caught, I will see that you receive in addition the reward offered by Colonel Fraser on behalf of the City of London Corporation. That reward is five hundred pounds.'

'For the chance of making six hundred pounds,' said Amelia, 'I'd act as bait to trap Old Nick himself.'

'You are sure that you realise the risk that you will be running?' I asked. I felt that it was only fair that she should be given every opportunity to express any doubts that she might have. 'As Mr Holmes said, we cannot guarantee your safety.'

She put down her coffee cup and said slowly, 'How many times, Doctor, have you told me that the Blue Ruin will be the death of me? And how many times have I told you that I only take the gin to give myself a little break from the worry of where the next meal is comin' from? Well, this is a chance for me to get out of Spitalfields and live somewhere decent. I am no longer a young woman and cannot work as well as I used to. The material of the trousers I make seems to get tougher and the needles blunter every year. It will not be long before I am unable to work at all. And what do I do then? Walk the streets? What other choice is there for a woman like me? The money you're offerin' is one way out; the only way. Yes, I know the risk but I'll take it. What do you want me to do?'

'I have in mind a scheme,' said Holmes, 'in which we find a way to make the killer believe that you know something of him – perhaps that you saw him with one of the victims and are able to identify him. You will have to spread this story when you are apparently the worse for drink. If, as I believe, the murderer is a local man, or at least a man with a room in the area, he will get to hear of it in fairly short order. He will then come and see if he can discover exactly what it is that you know. He will probably come and speak to you. When he does you will have to pretend to be a member of that class of women from whom he has drawn his previous victims. I will shadow you in case he has any ideas about attacking you in the street, though

I do not believe that he will. You will take him into your room and then Dr Watson and I will close in upon him and take him like a rat in a trap. The only problem to be solved is that of where the trap should be laid. We will need a room from which there is only one exit, though the plan will work if there are two.'

'If you think that an upstairs room that has only one door into it from the corridor and a window letting on to a closed court will suit your needs then the room I occupy in a lodging-house in George Street might do,' remarked Amelia.

'Capital,' cried Holmes. 'If our man checks up on you and learns that you have been in your room for some time past he will be less suspicious than if he were to discover that you had only just moved into the area. That only leaves the problem of how you could come to know what he looks like.'

'There may be a way to make that seem reasonable,' replied our visitor. 'I knew one of the victims and was amongst the last people to see her alive.'

'Indeed,' said Holmes eagerly. 'This is better than I had dared hope for. Which victim?'

'Annie Sievey.'

Holmes frowned. 'I recall no victim of that name,' he said.

'They said her name was Chapman at the court,' replied Amelia. 'I gave evidence to the coroner.'

'Of course you did,' said Holmes in a manner that suggested that he should have known this all along – though how he expected to be able to remember the names of all the witnesses in the case, I could not imagine. 'But did the newspapers not report your name as *Ann* Farmer?'

'Well,' replied our visitor, 'having two last names, I thought it was only fair that I should have two first names too.'

Holmes smiled and then began to pace swiftly about the room, muttering to himself and checking points off on his fingers. Finally he stopped and faced the two of us who had been watching him in silence, saying, 'Yes. It all hangs together. I think it will work.'

'What do you want me to do?' asked Amelia.

'For the moment, nothing,' said Holmes. 'Buy yourself some decent food and eat well for the next two or three days to build up your strength. Continue to frequent the public houses that you have patronised up to now but cut down on the amount of Blue Ruin that you drink; we'll need all our wits about us when we go into action.' Holmes stopped and walked over to his desk from which he took a small chamois bag which jingled as he tossed it in his hand.

'Here is ten pounds on account,' he said handing the bag to Amelia. 'The money is all in small coins – nothing larger than a florin – so that you will be able to spend it without anyone wondering where it came from. The good doctor and I will call on you tomorrow evening to spy out the lie of the land around your room. By then I will have thought out the way we will put the word about and draw the murderer to us. Until then I'll wish you good night.'

Holmes himself took Amelia downstairs and arranged for Billy to find a cab for her to take her back to the London. He was humming a glad air and rubbing his hands together with glee when he returned.

'A fine woman, Watson; a fine woman,' he said. 'I never cease to marvel that the appalling conditions that endure in the alleys and courts of our worst slums could still breed such as her.'

'You should be grateful that they do,' I said, 'for were it not for her desire to escape those alleys she would not put her life at risk by agreeing to aid you.'

'You are right, of course,' he said. 'But the fact remains that she is a brave woman. I am determined that no harm shall befall her while I am able to prevent it. We will go and scout her room, Watson, and if it is suitable we shall decide where you are to wait.'

'Wait?' I queried.

'I will disguise myself and shadow Mrs Palmer,' said Holmes. 'If the fiend takes our bait and she lures him back to her room I shall be just behind them. I will cover the door and you will watch the window. When they have had a few moments to get to know each other I will burst in upon them with a loaded revolver. He will either have to get past me, which he will not do, or throw himself through the window. If he lands in the court, Watson, you must shoot him with less compunction than you would feel had you to shoot a mad dog. You must give him no quarter.'

'You need have no fear,' I said. 'If he comes within range of my revolver he will not walk away unscathed.'

'Well said, Watson, well said.'

'One thing puzzles me—' I began.

'Only one?' asked Holmes with a smile.

'Why did you give Amelia so much money?' I asked, ignoring his sarcasm. 'If you only wanted her to eat well for a couple of days a pound or two would have been more than adequate.'

'I wished to see if she is trustworthy,' said Holmes. 'As I told her, we will need to have our wits about us and we cannot afford to have her the worse for gin. If she follows my instructions and cuts down the amount of spirit she imbibes we will know that she may be relied upon to carry out her part of the business. If we find her hopelessly drunk tomorrow then we shall have to reconsider our plan. That is why I gave her the money.'

I was about to make some remark to the effect that Holmes had given her so much money that she could be drunk for a month, but he did not give me time to speak.

'I believe that our fortunes in this case are about to turn,' he said. 'You have found a lure that I am certain will prove both reliable and effective. And when we get the Ripper under the muzzles of two revolvers, how can he escape?'

'He cannot,' I said, 'unless he has the luck of the devil.'

'He has had up to now,' said Holmes. 'Let us hope that he has used it all up.'

CHAPTER 8

Tethering and Beating

There had been much play made in the newspapers of the conditions that obtained inside the lodging-houses of the East End; those foul unhealthy hovels that were the nearest that the great majority of the metropolis's poor came to knowing a home. But no amount of editorial sabre-rattling, nor the occasional professional visit that I had made to such places, could have prepared me for the reality of the place where Amelia lived. Nobody could have called it home; of that I was sure. The entrance was through a narrow door with a great lantern over it. The lantern was so bright and so situated as to have two effects. It showed the location of the door the way a lighthouse shows the location of a rock and, while it lit up the outside of the house like a gin palace, it plunged the interior into a stygian gloom. But I knew that I would have to go inside since I had promised Holmes at breakfast that I would meet him here this afternoon. His optimism, which had been evident the previous evening following Amelia's visit, had somewhat diminished and he had decided upon the visit to see whether a night's sleep had caused Amelia to change her mind about participating in his scheme. I stumbled over the step and waited for a while to allow my eyes to become adjusted to the darkness.

After a few minutes I began to perceive that the passage in which I was standing led through to the back of the house. Not wanting to trust to my eyes without a little help, I struck a vesta and held it up to light the way. I wish that I had not done so. In the dark at least I could let my imagination colour the state of the building, allowing me to think of the paintwork with the odd peeling patch and the paper with an occasional tear in it.

In fact there was no paint and very little paper – on the wall, that is. There was more paper on the floor than there would have been if our landlady had left the heap that Holmes threw beside his armchair every morning for a month or so before she cleared it away. But what the walls lacked in paper they made up in other forms of decoration. There were cascades of water and lagoons of damp whereon mould had formed like slime upon the surface of a stagnant pond. And certain parts of the wall were moving! I held the match closer and saw that the reason for this was that there were groups of cockroaches scuttling back and forth across the walls. And, as if the walls were not bad enough, there was the floor.

I could hardly see the floor itself for the garbage that was strewn over it. Half-eaten bones and lumps of gristle, rotting cabbage stalks and potato peelings and other rubbish, indiscernible or indescribable. Scavenging cats rooted in the mess for edible tidbits and fought with the rats when they found them. That these battles were frequent and savage was shown by the number of corpses, both feline and rodent, that were lying about in various stages of putrefaction. And the smell! If it was true that a disease could be transmitted by its miasma then I would not be here to write these lines, for the stench was overpowering; a physical thing that reached out and coiled around you like an African python. I hurried towards the end of the passage as quickly as I could, scattering scavengers and rubbish at every step. Only a moment before my vesta expired, I reached the kitchen.

As I stepped into the crowded room, every eye in the place turned to stare at me and, as they took in my appearance, each eye held either resentment or animosity. There were about a dozen people in the room of whom four were men. They sat clustered around a fire that burned in the grate at one end of the room. A kettle steamed on the hob but I could see more beer jugs than tea cups in evidence. Aside from the fire a single candle lit the room and in its flickering light the faces of the men looked hard and brutal. One particular fellow lounged in the corner with a pint mug that might have held almost anything and watched me with a sneer. His face was swarthy and he had a vicious-looking knife scar that had been badly stitched running down one cheek. He scowled at me and then turned to spit into the fire.

'Whodja wan'?' he demanded in a low thick voice.

'What I want is no business of yours, fellow,' I said firmly. 'I am Dr Watson of the London Hospital and I am looking for a patient of mine. Do any of you know where I can find Mrs Palmer?'

There was a silence in the room for several seconds. When it became obvious that no answer was to be forthcoming I turned to retrace my steps into the passage to see if I could find the stairs myself. Amelia had said that her room was on the first floor and that it overlooked the court at the back of the house. I should be able to find her if I knocked on a couple of doors. As I started to leave the man who had spoken before spoke again.

'Where d'ja fink yer goin', Mister?' he growled.

'I told you before, it's "Doctor",' I said coldly, turning to face him again. 'And if you address me in that tone of voice you'll feel the weight of my fist against your chin.'

My outburst seemed more to amuse than to intimidate him. He chuckled vilely and stood up. I do not claim to be any braver than the next fellow but, by the same token, I trust I may say that I am no coward. However, as I watched him reach his full height I began to wish that I had brought my stick with me. He had three or four inches on me and was as bulky for his height as I am for mine. He drained his mug, belched enormously and said, ' So, ittsa boxin' match yer wan'in', is it?'

'A boxing match is a sporting contest between gentlemen,' I said. 'If I were to engage you it would be no more than a common brabble. Now, difficult though it is for me to tear myself away from your witty and erudite conversation, I must go and find my patient. If you'll excuse me.'

He did not give me time to turn away this time. 'I'm a-comin' wiv yer,' he announced. 'We don' wan' nobody pokin' aroun' wivvou' somebody ter keep anneye on 'em.' He seized the candle from the table and brushed past me into the corridor. Although his appropriation of the candle had left the kitchen in almost complete darkness not a single voice had been raised in protest as he walked out. I followed him into the passage and saw that just by the doorway into the kitchen there was a staircase. My guide turned and grinned at me. I tried not to look at the blackened and broken teeth that his grin revealed.

'The stairs is a bi' shaky,' he said. 'If yer keeps close ter the wa' yer mightn' fa' frough.'

Having given me this advice he sprang up the stairs with an agility unusual in one so bulky. I followed somewhat less quickly. Two or three times I felt the boards begin to give way beneath me but managed to get a foot upon the next step before I was pitched headlong into the stairwell. Eventually I reached the upper storey and rejoined my guide.

'Took yer bloomin' time, di'n't yer?'

'Which is Mrs Palmer's room?' I asked. I had no wish to become involved in another conversation with him.

He gestured down the corridor with the candle, which made the shadows dance, and said, ' 'Er room's a' the end of the passage.'

Without further ado he turned and strode down the corridor at such a pace that I expected the candle to be extinguished at each step. Surprisingly, it remained alight until we reached the door he had indicated. He rapped upon it savagely.

'Annie!' he roared. 'Yer've godda visitor.'

There was a pause before the door swung open and I saw the face of my patient peer out. She seemed relieved to see me but a little apprehensive to see that the ruffian from the kitchen was with me. From what I had seen of him I did not blame her for her apprehension.

'Isn't Mr Holmes with you?' she asked.

'I was about to ask you the same question,' I confessed. 'Mr Holmes said he would meet me here.' I hauled out my hunter and consulted it. 'It is unlike him to be late.'

'Nor is he,' said the ruffian beside me.

'What do you mean?' I demanded, wondering why he should

attempt to insinuate himself into our conversation.

'Come now, Watson,' he said, 'surely you can see through a little paint and grime?'

'Holmes?' I asked hesitantly.

'None other,' he laughed. 'Now, let us get inside the room before somebody spies our little conference.'

We entered my patient's room and closed the door at once. Amelia seemed at a complete loss at the sudden appearance of my friend. He read the consternation in her face and chuckled.

'You did not recognise me then, Mrs Palmer?' he asked.

'Indeed I did not, sir,' she replied. 'I had not expected to see you in such clothes; nor loafing in the kitchen as you have been all afternoon.'

'My dear lady,' exclaimed Holmes, 'I have been working all afternoon. In my new capacity as the keeper's helper I have been vetting all new arrivals. That is why I had to think twice before permitting you to enter, Watson. The house has certain standards to maintain, you know.'

'But what happened to Bruiser Bradshaw?' asked Amelia.

'You mean the hulking brute who used to hold the position that I now occupy? He and I had a discussion in the yard this morning over which of us possessed the better qualifications for the job. He advanced the argument of a haymaker that had all the subtle dexterity of a runaway pit car and I countered with a block and a jab to the solar plexus. Then I persuaded him with a hook to the point of his chin. After lying on the ground for a moment or two to consider, he decided that he would be better advised to seek employ elsewhere. So, I now help the keeper to ensure that only the most genteel of applicants are permitted to lodge here.'

'But why go to all that trouble?' I asked.

'So that I can be around when Mrs Palmer and her friend come in,' replied Holmes. 'You, Watson, will lurk in the dark corners of the court like a common felon to guard against the possibility of our man making an escape that way while I cover the corridor. In my "official" position I can come and go as I please. In no other way could I have so much freedom. Also I shall be able to accompany Mrs Palmer to the Ringer's for a "drop o' sommat wet" and a few words that will bring our prey to us.' He stopped and turned to face Amelia. 'That is, if you are still willing to go through with it?'

'Of course I'll go through with it,' she replied. 'I gave you my word, didn't I? Besides, I took your money so I can't change my mind, can I?'

'How much of the money do you still have?' asked Holmes.

'Nine pounds, eighteen shillings and eleven pence,' Amelia replied without a moment's hesitation. 'I spent sixpence on meat, fourpence on bread and tuppence on sugar. Then I decided to treat myself, so I bought a penn'orth of specks. Why? Wasn't I supposed to spend any of it yet? You can have the rest back if you want it. It's all here,' she added, reaching into a pocket hidden in her skirts. 'You can count it if you like.'

'You spent none on drink, then?' asked Holmes.

'No,' she replied. 'You told me to take it easy.'

'Excellent, my dear lady, excellent,' said Holmes. 'I really do believe that we three may carry it off between us. Since tonight is Friday I think that Amelia and I should start spreading the story of how she saw the fiend with Annie Chapman just before he lured her into the yard and killed her. It should not take very long for the story to get around. We will have to make the description detailed enough to make him think that we know exactly what he looks like.'

'But we don't know what he looks like, do we?' said Amelia.

'Yes, we do,' said Holmes. 'We have been told by a policeman that the murderer looks just like Dr Watson there. I've often thought that you had all the makings of a murderer, Watson. It's all there in your face. The cruel eyes; the sensuous lips; the imperious moustache; the pugnacious jaw; the animal strength of the muscular neck. It's all there.'

'So, you believe the young policeman's tale,' I said, ignoring his japing.

'Yes,' replied Holmes. 'He was convinced and his story had the ring of truth about it. So, Amelia, do you reckon that you can describe the good Doctor, here?'

'Yes,' she said. 'Without any problem.'

'Good,' said my friend. 'We'll go and sample the hospitality offered by Mrs Ringer's establishment. It would be unreasonable to expect any developments tonight, Watson. So, I suggest that you return to Baker Street. Wiggins has supplied me with a runner so that if anything should occur I can summon you at once.'

'I may be sure that you will do so should the need arise?' I asked.

'How can you doubt it, old friend?' said Holmes with more warmth in his voice than I was accustomed to hearing there. 'Be sure that when we spring our trap upon Jack you will be there.'

'I will go then,' I said.

'You might do well to spend your time sorting out some old clothes,' advised Holmes. 'In an area where cuffs are a luxury not often to be found,' he held up his own sleeves to show their ragged edges, 'your silk facings might attract undue attention. I will be back fairly soon. There is not a great deal that we will be able to achieve tonight.'

Seeing that I could do nothing to aid my friend at this juncture, I took his advice and returned to Baker Street; not without a little trepidation, however. Whatever Holmes's view of the likelihood – or rather, unlikelihood – of his coming face to face with the fiend during this particular night, I was still a mite concerned that he would not have anybody to call upon in a hurry should the need arise.

The need, apparently, did not arise. Dr Watson's diary contains no references to the Ripper murders until another two days had passed. The next incident concerning the hunt for the killer occurred on Sunday the 18th of November.

The time had got round to past eleven o'clock and I was thinking about turning in when I heard a cab draw up outside. The noise of the street door being flung open was followed by the sounds of somebody fairly bounding up the stairs. The door to the living-room was thrown open and Holmes rushed into the room with his thin face alight with the thrill of the chase. 'We have him, Watson; we have him!' he cried.

I started to my feet. 'You mean you've caught him?' I asked.

'I do not yet have him under lock and key,' confessed my companion, 'but I have every hope that I can rectify that deficiency in the immediate future. He's been asking after Amelia.'

'That was surely a little unwise of him,' I commented.

'It was Wiggins who spotted him,' replied Holmes. 'He was shadowing the lady and me on our way back to the lodging-house and Wiggins pretended that he knew Amelia and could tell him how to meet her.'

'Was he not suspicious?' I asked. It seemed to me that the fiend had exhibited a high degree of cunning up to now and the idea that he should so forego his usual caution as to ask about a proposed victim seemed unlikely, to say the least.

'Wiggins is a fluent liar,' said Holmes cheerfully. 'I coached him myself. He told the man that he was a junior member of the Old Nichol gang. He said that Amelia was going to be busy for the night, that is why I had accompanied her back to her room, but that he would arrange a meeting for tomorrow night. They'll meet in the Ringer's. He won't turn up to the meeting, of course; it is just a way of knowing where she will be at a particular time. Wiggins and I will have to keep our eyes open.'

'Did the man – er – resemble me at all?' I asked, recalling the scene with the young policeman.

Holmes's mouth twitched into a smile as he replied, 'Wiggins says that he almost gave the whole thing away by addressing the man as "Doctor". He says that he certainly looks like you at the first glance but that if you look closely you can tell that the other man is a little older, has a thinner moustache and is tanned to a colour several shades darker than our clime can produce – at least, in November.'

'A foreigner, then?' I said.

'He had an accent, according to Wiggins. The lad was inclined to put him down as an American.'

'That is promising,' I cried. 'There has been much

speculation in the newspapers that the fiend is an American. There seems to be an agreement that the two communications that appeared on the police poster contain a number of Americanisms.'

'Oh dear,' said Holmes. 'That's bad.'

'What on earth do you mean?' I asked.

'I have made it a rule that, in this particular case, whatever the newspapers say must be false. They have consistently advanced theories that have ranged from the inane to the impossible.' Holmes flung off his outer clothes and stood before the fire in his shirt-sleeves, absently rubbing his arms to warm them and staring into the flames. I was considering leaving him and retiring, thinking that he had fallen into one of his reveries from which it could take him anything from an hour to two days to emerge, when he shook himself like a dog climbing out of a cold stream. He turned to face me and I could see doubt in his eyes.

'Have I forgotten anything, Watson?' he asked. 'If I slip up this time I doubt that I will get another crack at him. I must not fail. I must not.'

'You will not,' I said firmly. I walked across the room to my desk and took out the brace of Webleys. I had cleaned and polished them so much during the past week that they shone like brilliants in the lamplight. 'These will ensure that you do not fail. One with me in the court and the other with you in the passage. I fear that they are not as accurate as your hair-trigger but rather more effective, I fancy.' I returned the pistols to their cases and mixed us each a whisky and soda. I carried them back to the fire and handed one to Holmes.

'It is not your habit to drink before you turn in,' he commented.

'A toast, Holmes,' I said ignoring his remark. 'The Whitechapel murderer safely behind bars.' I raised my glass.

'Amen to that,' said Holmes with rather more conviction than I would have expected from a man of his unconventional beliefs.

CHAPTER 9

Pit Fall

As will shortly become apparent, Dr Watson was unable to put on record an account of the encounter between Sherlock Holmes and Jack the Ripper that took place during the early morning of Tuesday the 20th of November 1888. The first published account, although the events are confused almost beyond recognition, appeared in the columns of The Times *of the 22nd of November 1888. In part the report read as below.*

Considerable excitement was caused throughout the East-end yesterday morning by a report that another woman had been brutally murdered and mutilated in a common lodging-house in George-street, Spitalfields, and in consequence of the reticence of the police authorities all sorts of rumours prevailed. Although it was soon ascertained that there had been no murder, it was said that an attempt had been made to murder a woman, of the class to which the other unfortunate creatures belonged, by cutting her throat, and the excitement in the neighbourhood for some time was intense. . . . The victim of this last occurrence, fortunately, is but slightly injured, and was at once able to furnish the detectives with a full description of her assailant. Her name is Annie Farmer, and she is a woman about 40 years of age, who lately resided with her husband . . . but on account of her dissolute habits, was separated from him. On Monday night the woman had no money, and, being unable to obtain any, walked the streets until about half-past 7 yesterday morning. At that time she got into conversation, in Commerical-street with a man, whom she describes as about 36 years of age, about 5ft. 6in. in height, with a dark moustache, and wearing a shabby black diagonal suit and hard felt hat. He treated her to several drinks, until she became partially intoxicated. At his suggestion they went to the common lodging-house, 19, George-street, and paid the deputy 8d. for a bed. That was about 8 o'clock, and nothing was heard to cause alarm or suspicion until half-past 9, when screams were heard proceeding from the room occupied by the man and Farmer. Some men who were in the kitchen of the house at the time rushed upstairs and met the woman coming down. She was partially undressed, and was bleeding profusely from a wound in the throat. She was asked what was the matter, and simply said 'He's done it,' at the same time pointing to the door leading into the street. The men rushed outside, but saw no one, except a man in charge of a horse and cart.

However, the day before this report was published Holmes was being called upon to explain what had happened. He received a terse note written on the stationery of the Diogenes Club which read as follows:

Sherlock,

    Come to dinner – eight o'clock.

                                 M.

CHAPTER 10

When Minutes Count

The document that follows was written at the instigation of Sherlock Holmes's brother, Mycroft. It is a transcript of a conversation that took place in the Strangers' Room of the Diogenes Club on the evening of the 20th of November 1888. Although the speakers are indicated by their initials only, their identities are obvious.

MH   This room is to be considered out of service until such time as we may have done with it. Have we all the necessaries? Then we need not detain you; we will serve ourselves. Sherlock, will you give our guest coffee while I hand out the brandy?

SH   I would willingly ask him how he takes his coffee were I to know by what name I should address him.

MH   You do not know him, then?

SH   Since you had already entered the dining-room by the time that I arrived and since the club's rule of silence prevented you from making any introductions I know nothing of him save that he is a son of the Duke of Pomfret, has but recently returned from the Orient, spends a great deal of his time hunting with a rifle and, before coming here this evening, he passed an hour in the *salles d'armes* with the foil.

LJR   What's this? Magic or mind-readin'?

MH   Neither. It is just my brother's way. He likes to dramatise the simplest observation.

LJR   Well, it don't seem simple to me, young fellah. How can you tell those things about me?

SH   They are really quite straightforward. The ring you wear upon your left hand has the Pomfret crest upon it. Only the Duke or a member of his family or household would wear such an item. Since you are too young to be the Duke, and I doubt that my brother's hospitality would stretch to inviting footmen to dinner, I'll hazard a shot at a son. The visit to the Orient is easy. The cigars you smoked during dinner were made in the Dutch East Indies. They are of poor quality and are not imported into this country so you must have brought them in with you.

LJR   Somebody could've brought 'em in for me.

SH   Indeed; but your tan is such as is not usually obtainable in England in November, which leads me to believe that you had brought them in yourself.

LJR   That was smart thinkin'. But how did you get the rest? How could you tell that I hunt with a rifle?

SH   From the lines around your eyes. The left eye is much more lined than the right, indicating that you screw up or close the left eye more frequently than you do the right one. I discarded the idea of a monocle since you are somewhat young for such a device and, in any case, I could see no sign of the instrument or of the need for it. So, why would a fit, active young man walk about with one eye closed? The answer is obvious. To enable him to concentrate on the view across the iron sights of his rifle.

LJR   I don't know about obvious. I suppose you worked out from the splinters in my left hand that I gained the final hit of my last bout with a *passata sotto*?

SH   No, that had escaped me, but I did note from the mark on your right wrist that your gauntlet is wearing through and is in need of replacement. You fence, I see, with the Italian foil and the handle has rubbed your wrist where it is held by the strap. You must either acquire a new glove or cultivate the French grip.

MH   If you have finished your exposition, Sherlock, perhaps we might move on to more important matters. Firstly, allow me to effect the introductions. Sherlock, this is indeed a son of the Duke of Pomfret, the third son, to be precise; Lord John Roxton. John, this is my brother, the famous detective, Sherlock Holmes.

SH   Well, your Lordship, how will you take your coffee?

LJR   Roxton, or Lord John, if you please. Black; anythin' else clouds the brandy—

MH   And this is a true Napoleon brandy – filched from the Emperor's own store by Lord Carey, father of one of the founders of the club.

SH   I presume that you invited me here for rather more than a passable meal and an exceptional cognac?

MH   I have a port, I thought you might appreciate . . .

LJR   I rather think you have been invited as an example to me.

SH   How so, Lord John?

LJR   I've been wond'rin' why your brother has fed and watered me as though I were his favourite doxy.

MH   Surely our friendship is sufficient reason?

LJR   Between yourself and my aged parent, perhaps. Don't misunderstand me; I'm grateful for the meal. I'd just like to know the price. I suspect it's to be a lecture along the track of 'Ain't-it-time-I-stopped-gallivantin'-about-the-globe-and started-makin'-my-way-in-the-world.' Am I right?

MH   Without giving the matter considerable thought I cannot imagine how you could have been more wrong. I was about to suggest that you might consider aiding my young and impulsive brother in his hunt for the criminal that the newspapers have named Jack the Ripper. If I were being pellucidly honest I might admit that your father did ask if I had any idea how to keep you occupied for a couple of weeks, until your boat sails for Brazil. I doubt that skulking about the stews of the East End after a mass murderer was quite what the old boy had in mind.

LJR   And what's your view of this proposed arrangement?

SH   It is all news to me. Perhaps you would care to explain, Mycroft.

MH   Very well. I asked you here this evening, Sherlock, for two reasons. Firstly, I want you to tell me why I should keep in idleness at my expense a woman my housekeeper thinks is a 'lady of the night'. Secondly, I want to know exactly what happened in the matter of Colonel Upwood. I have the misfortune to deal daily with an influential member of the Nonpareil Club and he is not entirely satisfied that justice has been done.

111

At this point a page of the manuscript is missing. By the time the memorandum resumes, the matter of Colonel Upwood and the Nonpareil Club has almost been dealt with and the conversation is returning to the subject of the Whitechapel murderer. The initial speaker is not identified but is obviously Sherlock Holmes.

. . . which could be substituted at an appropriate moment. Once the pre-arranged deck had been brought into play his success was assured. He knew the hands the other players held.

MH   Simple but brilliant. Now, about this woman you have decided I should entertain; who is she and why is she staying in my house?

SH   It is not safe for her to remain in London at the moment. She has been of the greatest assistance to me in the matter of the Whitechapel murders and, consequently, I believe she has been marked down for death by Jack the Ripper.

MH   Really, Sherlock, do try to sound a little less like your roommate. Who is she?

SH   Her name is Amelia Palmer – or possibly Annie Farmer: nobody seems to be sure.

MH   And for how long to you expect me to keep her as my guest?

SH   Until I have rid London of the Whitechapel murderer. Another day: two at the most.

MH   Really, Sherlock. There are times when I wonder how on earth you ever acquired a reputation for logic: simple coherence seems so often to elude you.

SH   Perhaps if you were to refill our balloons and listen for ten minutes without interruption I might be able to achieve some unity of narration.

LJR   If you two are goin' to go into the details of your police work it might be best if I bowed out and left you to it.

SH   On the contrary, I think that my brother's idea that you assist me with this case is an excellent one. Although I do not know you I am sure that Mycroft would not have recommended you had your courage and resourcefulness been open to question.

MH   There is indeed no question as to that. Lord John has not been long back from Shanghai. His activities whilst there caused him to come to the attention of the most powerful Tong in the city. Yet all their influence and terrible cruelty were not sufficient to prevent Roxton hunting down and killing five of their seven council members.

SH   And the other two. . .?

MH   Committed suicide to prevent further loss of life among the members of the Tong. They ordered that their heads be cut off and sent to Roxton as proof of their deaths. Only on receipt of those heads did he call off his vendetta.

LJR   I told you that story in confidence, Holmes.

SH   If you will agree to assist me you will learn a great many of my confidences and you may feel free to break those if you believe that Mycroft betrayed your trust lightly.

LJR   I don't think that for a moment. It's just that I don't see how I can help you. I wouldn't recognise a clue if it walked up and asked me for a light.

SH   After what I have just heard of you, I believe that you are the very man. However, it is necessary that you understand what has happened and how I became involved in the case in the first place before we discuss what is to be done.

Holmes describes his meeting with Major Smith and his subsequent activities up until the early hours of Tuesday the 20th of November 1888. Holmes explains how he had been following Amelia Palmer all night until. . .

. . . at about seven-thirty she was accosted by a man. I was unable to observe his features since he wore a low hat and a muffler. I trailed them to a public house where they had several drinks and where, as we had previously agreed she would, Amelia suggested that he should come back to her room in George Street. I was never more than twenty or thirty yards behind them all the way. As soon as they went into the house and up the stairs I ran out into the yard to ensure that Watson was there and was awake. I need not have worried. Then I made my way back to the landing outside Amelia's room.

I reached Amelia's door without a sound betraying my presence – I had previously noted which of the floorboards would not give me away – when I heard a sound that put all thought of silence out of my mind. It was the unmistakable noise of somebody being choked. The door was dry and worm-eaten and it yielded to my shoulder as though it were a sheet of glass. The noise and fury of my arrival froze the occupants of the room into a grim tableau.

Amelia, wearing only her under-garments, was half crouched upon the floor, her face white with fear and her eyes glazed. The man was hunched over her like a beast of prey. He looked up as I entered but I gave him no time to attempt any assault upon me. I produced my Webley and called upon him to give himself up. He reached under his jacket and pulled out a knife; but seemed to realise the inequality of the situation. His shoulders drooped and he released the pent-up breath he was holding and his right hand dropped until the point of the knife was level with his knees. Then, at the very moment when I thought I had him, he struck at me.

He suddenly whipped the knife from its low position, releasing it when the point was aimed at my heart. I whirled my free hand up in a semi-circular parry and squeezed the trigger at the same time.

LJR   Well, what happened?

SH   You will know that my defensive manoeuvre had been designed for those who habitually wear heavy gauntlets; without them it is painful indeed. The pain caused me to flinch and miss. The bullet intended to end the career of this fiend buried itself harmlessly in the wall of a common lodging house. Jack had no intention of letting me correct my marksmanship. He hurdled the iron-framed bed and smashed through the window, taking the sacking and the few remaining shards of glass with him. The wind of his passing extinguished the room's single candle but I could tell where to find Amelia by her laboured breathing, so I touched my fingers briefly to her throat. They came away dry. She was safe. I turned to follow the fiend through the window when

I heard Watson's voice from the yard. 'Stand or I fire.' As well command a charging elephant to halt. I threw myself through the window and as I did so I saw the yard illuminated by the flare of gunfire. For a moment I wondered why there should be such a pronounced echo in the yard. And then I realised why: I had heard the reports of two separate shots.

I could see the murderer about to run back into the house and as soon as I stopped rolling I cocked the revolver and loosed off a shot at him. I kept the trigger back, thumbed the hammer again and released it again – and then repeated the action. The three shots sounded almost as one; the sort of noise you hear when a boy runs his hoop-stick along a row of railings. But even so I missed.

MH   I always believed you to be something of a marksman, Sherlock; but I think I must revise that opinion. To miss with one shot might be regarded as unfortunate; to miss with three smacks of obstinacy.

LJR   Oh, come now, Holmes, that's not fair. Your brother was shootin' at a rapidly movin' target, instinctively, it would be too dark for him to see the sights of his revolver, and after he's just been wounded and had to throw himself head-first out of an upper floor window. It's no surprise that he missed. What was the man doin' while you were tryin' to pot him?

SH   He darted into the house, slammed the door and dropped the bolt. The door was rotten and it yielded to my second kick. I hurtled through the kitchen and the passage and out into the street.

MH   And. . .?

SH   Jack was nowhere to be seen.

MH   How. . .?

SH   He must have taken the short time he had while I was breaking down the door to compose himself and walk calmly away so that nobody even remarked him as he did so. I, on the other hand, was attracting a measure of attention. Aside from the stained and torn coat I had put on as part of my disguise as a loafer I had dirtied my face so that, what with the scar and the filth, it looked as vile as any you would find in the East End. Add to this a smoking revolver in one hand

	and a wound in the other that dripped blood on to the pavement and you may begin to envisage my appearance. There was a commotion in the house behind me and I heard a man call, 'There's a woman been attacked.' The crowd immediately assumed that I was responsible and I could see that unless I did something quickly I was going to be in some difficulty. I had but two rounds remaining in my pistol and, anyway, shooting uninvolved citizens was not the answer.
LHR	So that did you do?
SH	I pulled out my police whistle and blew several blasts upon it. As soon as it was answered the crowd began to melt away. Then I heard another man call from behind me, this time from the yard. 'Run for the barber,' he cried, 'there's a man bleeding here.'
MH	Watson?
SH	Yes. He'd been hit in the first exchange of fire. I rushed back through the house and out into the yard and could have cried for joy when I saw him.
LJR	But he'd been shot.
SH	Yes, but he was moving across the yard and that meant that he wasn't badly enough hurt to prevent him from trying to take a further part in the morning's events. He was lying on the cobbles half-way across the yard with his handkerchief tied tightly around his left thigh and his gun still firmly clenched in his right fist. He was inching himself slowly along the ground using his right elbow and leg. What a fellow he is. Badly shocked by the fiend's eruption from what I had confidently told him would be a foolproof trap and disabled in an exchange of shots, he had, nonetheless, patched himself up and was attempting to come to my assistance. And he wonders why it is I take him with me on my investigations.
MH	How badly is he hit, Sherlock?
SH	The wound itself is, I believe, not serious, but he has lost a great deal of blood. And his constitution has never fully recovered from the damage it sustained in Afghanistan.
MH	If you wish me to arrange for my own physician. . .
SH	That will not be necessary. I have already had Watson moved by special train down to Southsea where he may lodge with

Dr Conan Doyle who has attended him in a professional capacity before and who is, moreover, a friend. Billy has gone with him carrying my notes for Dr Doyle as to Watson's general health recently and how he came by his present wound.

MH   Then we may leave the good doctor in peace for the time being.

SH   I pray so; but I fear not.

MH   Explain yourself, Sherlock.

SH   While Watson and I waited in that foul yard for the doctor I had sent a man to fetch, I tried to force a few drops of gin – which was all that was to be had – upon him to ease his suffering. I marvelled that he was still conscious: the more so when I heard him say my name and something else that I could not catch. He reached up and pulled me down so that I might hear. . .

MH   We have no wish to pry, Sherlock, or to see a fellow at a disadvantage.

SH   No, what Watson had to say was important. I remember his every word. He said, 'Damnably sorry, Holmes . . . should've got him. Had a bead on him but . . . light from kitchen. Saw his face. Likeness. In my wallet . . . pictures . . ·San . . . cisco.'

MH   What did you understand by all of that?

SH   At first I supposed that his mind was wandering and that he was referring to the photograph of his late wife that he keeps in his wallet and whom he first met in San Francisco. But then he said, 'Last saw . . . other side . . . world . . .'

LJR   Fellah was obviously delirious. I've heard too many yellow-jack canzonets not to recognise one.

SH   That I do not doubt, Lord John. But this was no feverish hallucination. Watson had clung grimly to the vestiges of consciousness to try to tell me that which it must have broken his heart to reveal. It is no wonder that he broke down immediately afterwards.

LJR   What did he tell you, Mr Holmes?

SH   He revealed to me the true identity of Jack the Ripper.

MH   How could that gibberish have revealed anything to you?

SH	Because I know that while Watson may sometimes prate, he never gibbers. You need not press me, Mycroft, for I shall not disclose to you the name of the criminal: not yet, anyway. I hope that, with Roxton's help, I may terminate his murderous career but, if luck is with me, I may do so without having to reveal his name.
MH	Luck? For whom? And how can you be so confident that you will be able to bring the murderer to justice?
SH	Because I know his name, I know what he looks like and I know where he is known.
MH	Sherlock, it is your public duty to make these facts available to the police authorities and, in this instance, I nominate myself as their representative.
SH	No, dear brother, not even to you can I . . .
MH	Consider, Sherlock. Do you believe that Jack the Ripper will surrender himself to you without a struggle? I know that since your affray with the Amateur Mendicant society you consider yourself to be indestructible, but imagine the consequences were you to be struck down without having revealed the name of your assailant to any other.
SH	I have. That is why I have prepared this envelope for you; it contains my notes on the case and names the murderer. Before I hand it to you I must have your solemn promise that you will not open it unless you have incontrovertible proof of my demise.
MH	I give you my word as a servant of the Queen.
SH	Guard that manilla well: I shall expect it to be intact when I reclaim it. Come, Roxton, we'll away – unless you have doubts.
LJR	None. A suggestion, though: a stop at the Albany where I can change into some old clothes and collect my Adams.
SH	The clothes you will not need – I have your costume for the night – but the revolver is a useful thought. Good night, Mycroft, I shall communicate whatever news I have as soon as I may.
LJR	Goodbye, Holmes. Next time you invite me for a meal and a smoke I shall ask you to indicate whether you mean tobacco or cordite.

MH	Goodnight, Roxton; Sherlock. May God be with you.
SH	You have supplied me with Roxton and he and his revolver are all the company I require this evening.
MH	You may reveal yourself now, Sloane; they have gone. Had you any difficulties in recording the intricacies of the conversation?
S	No, sir, the Pitman's system of short-hand writing is both flexible and comprehensive.
MH	Have we a twin to this manilla about our offices?
S	Yes, sir, the very same.
MH	And can you duplicate the hand of this superscription?
S	Undoubtedly, sir. The writing is both firm and clear. A half-hour's practice should suffice to produce a counterfeit.
MH	Then we also may learn what my brother has learned.
S	But you gave your word —
MH	— that I should not open the letter; nor shall I. You will. What do you find?
S	Four, no five, octavo pages: but they are blank.
MH	Show me – some sort of secret writing, perhaps? No, these sheets are unmarked. What else is there?
S	Nothing. The envelope is empty.
MH	That makes no sense. Give it to me. I will hold it to the lamp. Hmm, I would lay odds that nothing, aside from my name, has been written here. But it feels stiffer than I would expect this type of manilla to be.
S	Stiffer, sir? What do you mean?
MH	That Sherlock has placed one envelope inside another and hidden his message between them. Here, slit the package open with your pen-knife. What do you find?
S	A cabinet.
MH	Show me.
S	Perhaps it is a picture of the murderer.
MH	That would seem to be the only logical conclu— Good God, it's Watson!

119

CHAPTER 11

Visitors to Baker Street

*This second memorandum is also written upon the stationery of the
Diogenes Club and is dated the day following the previous report:
the 21st of November 1888.*

MH Ah, Lord John; is Sherlock with you?

LJR No. He is to meet us here at nine.

MH Then we have a few minutes to wait. Since I have had no
word from my brother subsequent to our meeting yesterday,
I take it that no event of significance has occurred since then.

LJR Several events have occurred since then but I know nothin'
of their significance. What import do you give to the fact that
I have met and fought with Jack the Ripper?

MH I could assign no import to that at all until I knew the whole
circumstance. Give me the full details.

LJR Perhaps we should await Holmes – er, your brother?

MH I think we may settle upon Holmes. I am unlikely to become
confused whilst listening to your narrative. He has placed
restraint upon you? I thought not. Now, tell me what has
happened.

LJR Very well. As you know, we took our leave from here last
night in a cab. Holmes directed the cabbie to stop first in the
Albany outside my rooms and, since it is only a few minutes'
walk thence to Baker Street and he had some other
preparations to make, he took the cab on to his own
establishment. I stayed only long enough to equip myself
with my Adams and some spare ammunition and a small
flask and to instruct my man that he was to be ready to come
at my or Holmes's summons. He is an old campaigner and
may be relied upon. I did not bother to take a coat since

Holmes had informed me that he had my costume for the night.

It took me a very few minutes to complete my preparations and walk to Baker Street: and yet I was almost too late. As he had said he would, Holmes had retained the cab and it waited outside 221B. As I came alongside it I told the cabbie that I expected that we would be on our way shortly. He said it was goin' to be a bit of a squash, with the three of us. When I asked him what he meant, he said that the other gentlemen had arrived a minute or two previously. You don't hunt, do you, Holmes?

MH   Not animals.

LJR   Well, you'll may be have heard that a hunter develops a kind of sense of knowin' when his quarry's close by; perhaps laid up and waitin' for him. I had that sense then. I would have wagered my old Martini-Henry against a split Boxer case that the 'other gentleman' was our Jack of whom Holmes had told me in some detail durin' our drive from the club. I went into the house, drawin' and cockin' my Adams as I did so, and began to creep up the stairs. Feelin' mighty foolish, I might add. But I trust my senses and I'd rather get laughed at than shot at. As I made my way up the stairs I could hear two voices, one of which I could tell was Holmes's but all I could tell of the other was that it had a queer accent. I couldn't hear what was bein' said until I got to the landin' and – a fellah don't like to pry, but – I stopped outside the door and listened.

I heard Holmes askin' the other if he had known at whom he'd been shootin'. The other voice said that all it had been able to see had been the lamp and the gun and it had fired in between them. The man said he didn't know who it was until he read the papers in the morning. Even then, he said, he wasn't sure what had happened so he knew he'd have to come and talk to Holmes. He said he'd been waitin' about at the underground station for hours waitin' for Holmes to come back. But he'd known that it was really his lucky day when Holmes arrived and told the cabbie and his housekeeper that a man would be along directly. That's

121

when, he said, he'd realised that he could get in, deal with Holmes and be away before anybody could guess what he was plannin'. Holmes asked him what he *was* plannin'. The other replied that Holmes was the only person who knew who he was and that when he had put a bullet through his brain-case, he was safe.

Well, this told me that the man had a pistol and was intendin' to use it. The door wasn't shut, just pushed to – that's how I was able to hear what was goin' on – and I began to ease it open, little by little, so that I could spy out the lie of the land. As I was doin' this Holmes began speakin' again.

He said that John would know, and at first I thought he meant me, but I couldn't think what he was talkin' about. Then the other said that with Holmes dead and him disappeared, John would have no reason to say anythin' about it; always assumin' John did recognise him in the brief glimpse he would have caught in the flash of the pistols. He'd hardly want his relationship with him publicised, would he?

MH   Don't ask me. I am not sure that I know what you are talking about.

LJR   I think it becomes a little clearer in a while. Holmes asked if the other simply planned to disappear and the other said that he had already been in touch with his old connexions and hoped to hear by midnight that they had been able to secure a passage for him. Within a month he'd be on the other side of the world. No one would be able to find him then. Holmes asked him why he was goin' to kill him – Holmes, that is – if he was safe; after all, he couldn't reveal the other's identity without the news gettin' to John and that intelligence would probably kill him. Holmes pointed out that if he couldn't find the man and couldn't denounce him he posed no threat. The other man said that John had told him that Holmes was the cleverest man alive and he wouldn't have him on his trail.

I heard the unmistakable double click of a revolver bein' cocked and knew that, whether or not I could see into the room, I was goin' to have to make my move soon.

Holmes was as calm as you please and asked the man, before he killed him, to answer three questions. The man agreed. Firstly, Holmes asked him his name 'You mean you really don't know me?' he asked. Holmes said that he knew the man was Dr Watson's brother and that to the world at large he was known as Jack the Ripper, but that was all. The other man said that his name was Henry Watson and supposed that his physical resemblance to his brother had given him away. Holmes said that it was and then asked him why he committed the murders. There was a long pause durin' which I was able to get the door open far enough for me to see the speakers. Holmes stood by the mantelpiece with his back to the fire; it was quite obvious to me that he had been able to see the door openin' and I wondered whether he had started askin' the questions just to keep Jack talkin'.

Jack was talkin' again now and sayin' that he couldn't even tell himself why he did the things he did, much less anybody else. He doubted that Holmes could understand the feelin's of loathin' and disgust he suffered after each event: or of the need that drove him beforehand. Holmes said that he'd seen what he'd done to one of his victims and if he could infer the impetus from the result then he thought he might have some idea of the forces drivin' him.

I could see the other man – Henry Watson – now. He stood half-turned from me facin' Holmes. His left side was towards me so I could not see the gun I knew he held. Holmes asked him why he had killed Mary Jane, whoever she might be, because he – Watson – had known her. Watson replied that he had known them all; how else did he think he'd been able to persuade them to go into dark squares and back-alleys with him?

I don't look upon myself as a cold-blooded man but I hope I may say that I know where my duty lies. I had heard this man admit to bein' a killer and I had heard him threatenin' to put a shot through Holmes's skull. I knew what I had to do and so I took my stance and presented my Adams. I would have to make a clean kill; givin' him no chance of gettin' off a shot. I had got my aim and was slowin' my breathin' when there came a most surprisin' distraction.

MH   For Heaven's sake, Roxton; don't stop now.

LJR   Sorry, Holmes. I'm just gettin' my thoughts sorted into order. Everythin' seemed to happen at once. There was a piercin' shriek and a crash of dropped crockery. My nerves were pretty keyed up and I loosed off the shot I'd been aimin' – straight through the window. I looked down to the foot of the stairs and saw that Holmes's housekeeper had been in the act of bringin' up a tray of coffee when she had caught sight of me drawin' a bead, as she thought, on her tenant and had screamed. I snapped my head back round and saw that the interruption had had a dramatic effect on the occupants of the room. The combination of scream and shot had totally unnerved Watson. He was comin' through the doorway at me like a huntin' leopard. Holmes had whirled about and wrenched a knife from the mantel, scatterin' paper as he did so, and was shoutin' at the top of his voice, 'It's all right, Mrs Hudson; he's a colleague.'

      By now Watson had crashed into me and precipitated the pair of us, in an intertwined *mêlée* of flailin' limbs, down the stairs. My gun got caught between the banisters and torn from my grasp; his, I never saw the goin' of, though Holmes later found it upon the landin'. We tumbled to a halt at the bottom of the stairs. Jack was on top and he gave me a fist to the side of the head that I knew nothin' of until it arrived. I closed a hand around his ankle but he scrambled to his feet and delivered a kick to my ribs with his unencumbered foot. Then he was up and headin' for the street door. I saw him brush Mrs Hudson aside and I heard Holmes cry, 'Shoot, Roxton! Shoot!' I hadn't even the breath to tell him I had lost the gun.

      Holmes sprang down the stairs, leapt me like a 'chaser and shot down the passage like an express running ten minutes behind schedule. I eased myself up into a sitting position and asked Mrs Hudson if she was all right. She replied that she was only a little taken aback and asked if I knew whether Holmes was goin' to be back that night and should she prepare another pot of coffee. Before I could answer her, Holmes came back. He helped me to my feet and began to fuss over me until I demanded to know what had happened outside the house.

He gave a wry smile and told me that Watson had simply climbed into the waiting cab and told the driver to whip up and be off.

MH Whatever else you may say about this man there is no doubt but that his nerves are of the first order. What happened then?

LJR Holmes quietened Mrs Hudson and told her not to worry about another pot of coffee since we would soon be on our way. He also despatched the boy to secure a new cab. He took me back upstairs, found Watson's dropped revolver and poured us both a generous measure while he rehearsed to me his plans for the evenin'. Before he could say very much I interrupted him by askin' him how he thought our recent brush with the murderer would affect our chances of being able to secure the fellah. I was much surprised when he said that he thought it would make it easier to lay hands upon him.

I asked Holmes what he meant, pointin' out that he was goin' to be even more on his guard now that Holmes had beaten him square twice and if I were puttin' money on it, it would be on him cuttin' and runnin'. Holmes asked what I meant by his havin' beaten Jack twice so I told him that he'd stopped Jack rippin' up this Mrs Palmer he'd told me about and Jack had been all set to put a bullet through Holmes's brains and he'd been blocked again. I said I thought he'd been lucky so far and that he wouldn't be makin' any moves for a while yet. He'll lay up in the long grass and wait till things have calmed a little.

Holmes shook his head and said that Jack had already told him that he was plannin' to leave the country, and Holmes had no reason to believe that he would not do so. I reminded him that both he and I knew who Jack was and he must know we would give him away. Holmes shook his head again and said that if we gave Henry Watson away the publicity would very likely kill Dr Watson since, in his own medical opinion his health is irretrievably ruined and the emotional strain,

125

comin' on top of the physical shock, might well complete the task the bullet began. Watson, *Henry* Watson, would gamble on Holmes doin' nothin'. 'But we must do somethin', Holmes,' I said. 'We can't let him get away.'

Holmes said that he had no intention of lettin' Watson get away; he reminded me that I'd said that I wouldn't recognise a clue if it came up and asked me for a light and said he'd like to see what I made of somethin'.

He produced a knife from a drawer and handed it to me with a small laugh saying that he'd have to start a museum of weapons he had collected from Jack the Ripper, what with the knife as well as the pistol. This was the knife Jack had thrown at Holmes in Mrs Palmer's room. I hefted it and looked it over for a minute. It wasn't a fightin' knife; blade wasn't wide enough, makin' it too fragile in the thrust to use in a real rough-and-tumble. It looked as though it would cut through flesh pretty easily, though. I ventured the opinion that it was some kind of butcher's knife.

Holmes suggested I look at the point. I did so and saw at once that the point had been discoloured; the blade had been held over a flame at some time. Holmes revealed that the discolouration was due to more than the heat of a flame alone. He prised a dark speck of somethin' from the knife and handed it to me. I looked at it and recognised it as the remnant of an opium dottle. I asked Holmes what significance he read into it. He reminded me that opium smokin' is not usually a solitary vice; smokers meet and smoke at a divan which, among its other amenities, provides an individual known, I believe, as a chef, whose function it is to knock out and recharge the patrons' pipes. He has his own equipment for doin' this. The fact that the owner of the knife had had to perform these functions himself indicated two things to Holmes; one, that he is addicted to the drug and two, that he had had to abandon his usual haunts and provide for himself in private.

MH   Why should he do that?

LJR   I asked the same question. Holmes suggested that Watson might have been afraid that he would give himself away in his incoherent ramblin's.

MH	So, Sherlock proposes to track him through the dens, does he?
LJR	That also was my thought; but it was not Holmes's – he was of the opinion that we would have to try only one.
MH	But, there must be thousands of the places in London.
LJR	Some hundreds, anyway, according to Holmes, who asked me how many I knew by name. I knew the name of one only, the Bar of Gold in Upper Swandom Lane. Holmes nodded and asked me how I came to know of the second most infamous divan in the metropolis. I had to stop and think at that. Eventually I recalled bein' told of it by one of the Chinese galley skivvies on the Bombay Packet. Holmes was not surprised, telling me that I had been told of the Bar of Gold because I was comin' from the east and the Portuguese who owns the place has his connexions in that direction. Had I travelled from the New World, I would have had the T'ien Shen, or Spirit of Heaven as it is more commonly called, recommended to me. And Holmes believes that Henry Watson arrived in this country from San Francisco.
MH	And Sherlock hopes that the people at this place will tell him where he may find Watson?
LJR	More than a hope, apparently. Holmes avowed his intention of confrontin' the owner with the plain fact that if they did not assist him they were not much longer to remain in business.
MH	What was to be your role in this affair?
LJR	When I asked that question of Holmes, he bent to another cupboard and produced a tube of wood about half an inch in diameter and eighteen inches long and a small tin. He asked me if I could use it. I opened the tin and saw the tiny, feathered darts and told him, yes, I can use a blow-pipe. When I asked him how he'd come by it, he said shortly that it had belonged to an Andaman Islander. He paced about a bit as though checkin' through his thoughts and then turned and faced me square.

He reckoned that this was not a time for lengthy deployment of forces. If we were to be successful, he told me, we must act now; boldly and decisively. He would make a frontal assault to flush the fugitive and I must be the gun in the hide. Holmes looked grave as he told me I must not fail; when the felon came within range of my pipe I must have him. A second of hesitation could prove to be fatal as it so nearly had done with Watson. I reminded Holmes that I had heard our quarry threaten him and boast of his crimes: I would have no doubt.

He simply grunted and said that now we had to turn our attention to changin' me into a Chinese servant – though I pointed out that with my blue eyes and red hair, he was goin' to have the devil's own job to do.

But do it he did: and when he had finished I was a regular Boxer – pig-tail and all. Then we were off. As the cab – the new one found by the boy Holmes despatched for that purpose – tumbled us about, Holmes outlined his stratagem for the capture of Watson. We clattered through Marylebone, Bloomsbury, Holborn, the City and the edges of Whitechapel. Eventually we were set down in the East India Dock Road; the heart of Limehouse. I found it all rather disappointin': there was no sign of any dope orgies nor any hint of white slavin'. I told Holmes that I supposed we had come upon a slow day but he informed me that Limehouse was, by comparison with its neighbour, Whitechapel, a model of sobriety and orderliness.

SH   But these things are all relative, Roxton.

MH   Sherlock, you come most carefully upon your hour, as usual.

SH   I have always found that punctuality is as disquieting to a public servant as is polygamy to a missionary; since human nature ever distrusts that with which it is unfamiliar. Indeed I would have been here earlier had it not been for the fact that I raided your cellar. I have two of the Margaux '64, bottled on the estate.

MH   I trust you have some valid cause for your celebration.

SH   Not one cause, brother, but two. Here, Lord John, you have a swordsman's strength in the wrist. Turn to and open one of these.

MH   I fear I cannot join you if you wish merely to laud the termination of a criminal's career, however notorious he may have been.

SH   Then join me in celebrating the deliverance of a friend and colleague of whose life I had despaired.

MH   You have had some news of Watson, then?

SH   I have been to Southsea and have spoken to Dr Conan Doyle and I may say that I now share that gentleman's optimism that all will be well with my fellow lodger.

MH   I had hoped that you had come to speak of weightier matters.

SH   And so I have. Roxton and I have come to tell you of the end of Jack the Ripper; and of the part that you must play in it.

CHAPTER 12

Deep Waters

MH	My part? Do you mean to tell me that this murderous fiend is still at large?
SH	No, he is quite abridged now – as you will know if you will but sit and listen for a quarter of an hour. Thank you, Lord John. What point had you reached in your narrative?
LJR	I had just spoken of our arrival in Limehouse last night.
SH	You have told Mycroft of our encounter with the killer and of the fact that I owe you my life?
LJR	I have told him that I managed to frighten your landlady and gouge a rut in one of your banisters.
SH	Such self-effacement is worthy of Watson himself. But, Limehouse. Limehouse is considerably more respectable than some of its neighbours but I was nonetheless glad of the fact that I had a companion with me as we made our way towards the Cut; that torpid stretch of grey water that is both the geographical and, in the strictest sense, ontological centre of the locality.
MH	Please, Sherlock, give me merely the facts. I can wait until the next Beeton's for the illustrated edition.
SH	Very well, then; the facts only. My card gained us entrance to the divan of Ah Cheong, as I had supposed it would since we have had dealings in the past. Before my interview I requested that Roxton, who was impersonating my deaf-mute servant. . .
MH	Deaf-mute?
SH	It is a role that I had originally conceived for Watson: there is a limit to his dissembling. Roxton was led away into the darkness of the back of the building, there to be provided with a pannikin of water, whilst I talked to Ah Cheong.

MH   And this – Ah Cheong? – did he agree to help you?

SH   He? Ah Cheong is the second cleverest woman I have had to do with and the only person of her sex to have blocked me twice – though once was by luck only. Her apartments, which are above the divan, are both an education and an inspiration to the student of the Orient. For example, in her receiving room there is a small opium table upon which stands a collection of jade miniatures, mostly workman-like Han pieces but with an exquisite representation of Fu-hsi that I would say was pre-Imperial Chou. . .

MH   I shall wait until Watson is recovered and ask him to provide me with the facts of the matter. Not even he could embellish a simple narrative in the way that you are doing.

SH   I talked to Ah Cheong and tried to persuade her that it would be in her interest to assist me. Eventually I had to suggest to her that if she did not agree to aid me then a bundle of her letters – what one might call, with some justification, animated correspondence with the master of the *Matilda Briggs* – might come into the possession of the authorities.

MH   Surely that hapless vessel was lost at sea in mysterious circumstances some years ago. How could letters written before that event influence a decision that had to be made now?

SH   Ah Cheong made much the same point, and I gave as the reason the light those letters throw on the behaviour of a Mr van Erp who is a director of the Netherlands-Sumatra Company. Surely, you recall the newspaper reports of the proceedings at that company's extraordinary Extraordinary General Meeting? Those events are somewhat more recent. Ah Cheong recalled them only too well. I suspect that she only asked the question in order to test whether I really was *au fait* with the letters' contents.

Eventually, she asked me what it was I wanted to know. I told her that I believed that Henry Watson had been in contact with her, seeking passage out of the country; possibly to San Francisco. I had expected that she would have to contact some of her people before she could provide an answer, but I was wrong. 'Mr Watson is known to me,' she

131

said. 'He has smoked here, no doubt?' I said. 'My relationship with my clients is as professional as your own, Mr Holmes,' she said, 'and as confidential.' She took up a silver bell from her desk and rang it gently.

MH   Your recollection of these conversations seems sometimes little short of marvellous.

SH   It is merely something that I have disciplined myself to do. My memory is such that it does not retain that which passes through it for more than a few days; but during those few days its contents are available for my review *in toto*. It has been part of my training. But, to continue: at this point, an elderly Chinese entered the room and kowtowed; Ah Cheong spoke rapidly to him in Cantonese and dismissed him. She told me that she had asked her servant to find out what arrangements had been concluded with Henry Watson. I knew that she had also ordered tea to be brought. A few minutes went past during which we spoke of the occasions in the past when our paths had crossed and then the servant returned. It transpired that Watson was due to return to the divan at midnight with the money to pay for his passage.

I consulted my watch. It lacked twenty minutes of midnight. Ah Cheong suggested that we have tea served and I agreed. We spent a most stimulating quarter of an hour ranging over a number of diverse subjects including the anthropological relationship between the Chinese and *Equimaux* races, the development of the oriental man-bearing kite into an independent powered flying-machine, the culinary use of toads and other amphibians and the problems of working jade: Ah Cheong spoke of each as though she had made a special study of it.

It was four or five minutes before midnight when the ancient servitor reappeared with the intelligence that Henry Watson had returned and, in accordance with the suggestion I had previously put to Ah Cheong, had been asked to wait upon the embankment that abutted the rear of the premises. As I rose to leave, Ah Cheong looked at me and said, 'There is one favour that I would ask of you, Mr Holmes. I have no knowledge, nor do I desire any, of your reasons for pursuing your quarry but I do have some knowledge of his character and I do not believe that he will go with you quietly. If there must needs be violence I would prefer that it be not on my premises.'

I drew out my revolver with the intention of loading the chamber that I had left empty but Ah Cheong placed an absolute prohibition upon the use of firearms, explaining that there had recently been an incident involving two American sailors settling old scores which had ended in shooting. Ah Cheong had been warned that any repetition of the incident would result in her divan being closed down. I explained that the revolver was merely for insurance in the event that the quieter method I proposed to try first should fail. She accepted this but then added a warning, 'Should the letters of which we spoke earlier ever come to light I shall know who was responsible. The Sage has said, "The runner may be netted; the swimmer may be hooked; the flyer may be felled with a corded arrow." You would do well to bear such considerations in mind.'

'As I recall,' I said, 'Confucius spoke those words after his meeting with Lao Tzu; and it was the latter who said, "He who excels at tying uses no cords, but what he has knotted cannot be undone." You would do well to bear that in mind.'

'I think it may be said that we understand one another,' said Ah Cheong. 'I bid you "Goodnight" and trust that I may not be thought rude if I say that I do not wish to see you again.'

I merely bowed and followed the old servant out of the room. He led me through a maze of corridors and passages until we reached a door which he threw open. I stepped on to the very bank of the river.

It was a beautiful night, clear and calm and with only the merest edge of cold. The view along the river to Shadwell and Bermondsey with the riding lights of the dozens of anchored craft bobbing and blinking in the flow and eddy of the tide seemed to me to greatly resemble Grimshaw's 'Nightfall Down the Thames'. I had, however, little time to appreciate the beauties of the night. I left the door behind open so that my features would be in shadow and my recognition delayed until I had been able to close with him. But in this hope I was to be frustrated. I saw the figure of Watson staring down into the dark waters of the river. I could not see Roxton but that did not greatly surprise me.

LJR   You had told me to conceal myself. And, anyway, I gave the pibroch of the whaup as soon as I saw you.

SH   Possibly it was the sound of the birdsong that caused Watson to turn and face me. 'What ship?' he called eagerly, taking a step forward. 'And whither bound?'

Something, perhaps my lack of response or his familiarity with my shape alerted him and I heard his sharp intake of breath. 'The game's up, Watson,' I said. 'You must surrender yourself to me.' He growled a curse and snarled, 'Never. You have interfered once too often, Holmes.' His hand snaked inside his jacket and I had no doubt that he was seeking a weapon. I curled my fingers around the butt of my revolver, but I did not draw it.

I knew that I could not shoot him; the resulting publicity would be far too intense since, whatever the social reformers might claim, murder by shooting is sufficiently uncommon, even in Limehouse, to attract a deal of attention. My name alone would be enough to provoke the interest of the newspapers and my involvement in the shooting of my room-mate's brother would be irresistible to them. I had hoped to get close enough to him to cover him effectively with the pistol, but I had not done so. If he pulled a gun now I might be forced, in spite of everything, to shoot in self-defence. Watson's hand reappeared: empty. He had evidently been unable to replace the revolver he had lost in the scuffle with Roxton at Baker Street. He had reached for the gun with his left hand and now the wan light from the door behind me fell across his open palm. I could plainly see, even in the poor light, the puckered scar to which the young constable had alluded. Watson, seeing that I had not drawn my own pistol and perhaps sensing my impotence, turned and ran to the very edge of the river-bank.

There were, I knew, any number of craft on the river and

once Watson got amongst them he would be lost to us for good. He could be out of the Metropolis and then there would be no way in which I would be able to trace him. I could not ask the police, or anybody else, for help since the risk of Henry Watson's secret becoming common knowledge was too great. I had to stop him now. Out of the corner of my eye I could see a dark shape that was Roxton rearing himself up from behind some stacked crates. In one hand he held a long thin tube and the other hand was in the act of covering the tube. He had loaded a dart into the pipe. But he would not have time to aim and fire because Watson was in the very act of casting himself over the low stone wall that bordered the river. He would be gone unless I could delay him for long enough to enable Roxton to draw a bead. I had an idea.

LJR   Gave me a nasty jolt, I can tell you.

SH   A voice sounded from just within the opened door to Ah Cheong's divan: the voice of Dr John H. Watson. 'Henry,' it said, 'for God's sake wait, man! We can work something out.'

MH   But, Watson's in Southsea.

SH   I have perfected a small skill in ventriloquism and you should recall that I was always something of a mimic. In any event, my shout had the effect of causing the fugitive to pause, crouched on the wall, unsure whether to follow his ears or his instincts. Then, without a word, he turned and plunged into the dark waters beneath him. I sprinted to the wall and stared down but could see nothing. Roxton dashed up and joined me, stuffing another dart into the pipe. 'Did you hit him?' I asked. 'Couldn't tell,' he said.

LJR   Shot at him but he dived over the wall so dam' fast I couldn't see if I'd got him or not.

SH   A light had appeared on the deck of a barge which had been moored for the night thirty yards or so from the bank. In the wan circle of light cast by a hooded lantern I could see the dark, sleepy face of a seaman and loosely furled sails. 'Deck there,' I called, 'man overboard!' My use of the time-honoured formula for a man in distress acted like a pan of

135

iced water thrown into the face of the mariner. He wrenched the hood off his lantern and played the beam across the black surface of the water. Almost at once he picked up our quarry.

Watson floated, face down and immobile, just a yard from the bank of the river. In the wash of light from the lantern I could see that there was a flight of greasy stone steps leading down to water level. The top of the steps would be about twenty feet along the bank from where we stood. By now the sailor had spotted the floating figure. 'There 'e is,' he yelled at the top of his stentorian voice. I turned to Roxton. 'You'd better get back under cover. That shout is bound to bring out the idlers. When there's something of a crowd you will easily be able to mingle with them. Stay close to me; Ah Cheong as good as threatened me with violence if anything should attract attention to this place. I have an idea or two that might serve to make this seem no more than another riverside tragedy.'

I climbed over the wall and descended the slippery steps. At the bottom there was a small landing stage and attached to a corroded iron ring set into the wall was a length of greasy cable. I quickly fashioned a noose and cast it at the floating figure which had still not moved. At my third cast I secured the noose around a drifting limb and it was then the work of a very few seconds to haul the body ashore. As soon as I felt the dead weight of the man I judged that he was no longer alive. I turned him over and knew at once that there could be no doubt. One side of his forehead was caved in. He must have hit the side of the riverbank or some submerged rock as he had dived in. Just above his collar and below his ear, in the small exposed section of the jugular vein, was the poisoned dart that Roxton had shot at him. I removed it and secreted it in my matchcase. Whether the dart or the fall had killed him, or whether the one had led to the other, I did not know. A quick but thorough search through his pockets revealed that the only items upon his person that might identify him were his wallet and his watch, which was inscribed with his initials. Both of these items I removed from the body. The longer the time before his identity were established, the less the likelihood that my presence at his death would be remembered. I had a hip-flask of brandy – association with Watson has taught me some of the tricks of the medical profession – and I forced a few drops between his unresponsive lips and spilt a little more down the front of his already sodden shirt.

' 'Ow is 'e, mate?' called the bargeman. 'I'm afraid he's a goner,' I called back. As though this statement ended any interest that he might have had in the matter he rehooded his lantern and went back below. However, I was not left in the dark very long. The beam of a lamp held by one who stood at the top of the steps was played over me. 'What's goin' on down there?' demanded a gruff voice. 'Just fished a dead 'un out of the river,' I replied. 'A jumper?' asked the unseen owner of the voice. 'I don't think so,' I said. 'If you could smell him I think you'd agree he probably just slipped and fell.' 'I'd better come down, then,' he said.

There was a pause broken only by the sounds of a man unused to exerting himself and then a large, middle-aged policeman stood beside me. He played the beam of his bull's-eye over the features of the dead man, winced as he took in the battered forehead and bent to smell the wet clothes. 'I guess you 'ave the right of it. 'E stinks worse'n a paid-off clipper 'and. You see it 'appen?' 'No,' I confessed. The policeman regarded me in a none too friendly way and said, 'I think you'd better tell me 'oo you are an' what you're doin' 'ere.' I handed him one of my cards and he turned his lamp upon it. 'Sherlock 'Olmes,' he read. 'I've 'eard of you, Mr 'Olmes. Was you down 'ere on p'lice bus'ness?'

I told him that I was not but had been here only to indulge my taste for a pipe or two. He accepted that explanation and turned his attention back to the corpse. 'Did 'e jump or did 'e just fall?' he mused. 'If I might have the loan of your lamp for a few moments, we might be able to discover which,' I told him. He handed his bull's-eye to me and I made a deal of fuss over examining the dead man's boots. Then I led the way back up to the bank where a sizeable crowd had now gathered. I walked along beside the wall shining the light upon it. Eventually I came to the spot where Watson had stood, briefly, on it. I peered closely at the top of the wall there and invited the policeman to do likewise. 'I'm sure that what took place here is now as plain to you as if you had been a spectator,' I said, 'but, perhaps, you will allow an amateur to offer his own comments?' He indicated that I should go ahead.

'You undoubtedly noticed the unusual arrangement of nails in the heels of the dead man's boot,' I said, 'and saw at once that at some time in the past they had been repaired by a cobbler who had used proper hob-nails but that, more recently, someone, doubtless the owner, had repaired them himself, using small coach nails. Such a combination is rare and we may assume that the configuration in which they occur is so rare as to be virtually unique.

'Now, we may ignore the cobbles here since they are too hard to be marked by the nails of a man's boots. The flags on top of this little wall, however, are considerably softer and you may plainly see, here, and here, the marks of the nails. There are only a few scuffs so we know that the man did not stay long upon the wall; so it is unlikely that he stood for a period making up his mind to jump as, I think, is usual for those who decide to fling themselves into the water. Is that not so?' 'Aye, sir, so it is,' he agreed. 'So,' I said, 'we know that the man stood upon the wall for but a short time. Now, consider these semi-circular scratches here. How could they be caused but by the man swinging himself suddenly round from facing the river to face this way? And the cause of this rapid whirl? I am afraid that I must have been the cause. Having had my pipes I stepped out for some air and in flinging open the door I alarmed our river-gazer. He swung violently around and, not being altogether sober, he missed his footing – you can plainly see the scrape here as his left foot slid from beneath him – and plunged into the water.'

'And the blow to the head, sir?' asked the policeman. 'I can but conjecture that he hit the riverbank or some submerged rock when he hit the water,' I said dismissively. 'I couldn't've put it better myself,' responded my colleague.

'It was this door 'ere you said you flung open, wasn't it?' I nodded. 'So, all we need is for somebody to confirm that you was in that place earlier tonight an' we can all go 'ome.'

I was somewhat perturbed by this turn of events. I had given my word to Ah Cheong that I would not bring her establishment into the night's events and I had hoped the policeman would not look too closely into the story I had told him. I wanted this affair to be over and done with now; and for nobody to think that it was anything more than an unfortunate accident. Sherlock Holmes happening to be on hand when an unidentified man fell into the river was one thing, but Sherlock Holmes lying about his involvement in the death of his best friend's brother was quite another. I did not like to think what the more unprincipled newspapers would make of that.

The policeman started towards Ah Cheong's back door but before he had covered half the distance a ragged figure skulked out of the door, sidled over to me and plucked at my sleeve accusingly. 'You no pay,' the figure whined. 'You smoke much pipe and you no pay.'

Before I could think of anything to say the policeman beside me chuckled and said, 'Well, sir, that seems to settle that. I 'ope you 'aven't took no offence at my checkin' on your story, Mr 'Olmes. You can't be too careful.' 'I quite agree,' I said. 'My address is on the card if I can be of any further assistance in this matter but,' I dropped my voice to a conspiratorial whisper, 'I'd be obliged if my name could be kept out of this matter: I am engaged in one or two rather delicate cases at the moment and would prefer not to have my name linked to a tawdry business like this.' 'Then, I suggest you cut along, sir,' he said. 'I can 'andle things 'ere. You'd better pay that 'eathen off before 'e tries pullin' a knife on you.' 'I'll do that now,' I said. I turned to the menial from the divan to get him to take me back in, still supposing him to have been sent by Ah Cheong in order to smooth things over as rapidly as possible, and received a considerable surprise when I caught sight of his face in the light from the open door. It was Roxton.

LJR   Didn't think I was goin' to start play-actin' too, did you?

SH   Indeed, I did not. But it was quick thinking on your part and it saved some awkward questions. After that there seemed little point in remaining in the vicinity so we set off at a brisk pace. With Roxton dressed like a music-hall conjuror it took us a while to find a cabbie who was prepared to take us on but eventually we arrived home.

LJR   Holmes, we have murdered a man.

SH   Not murdered, Roxton; executed. There's a world of difference.

LJR   Is there no chance of an error? Is there no hint of doubt in your mind?

SH   None at all. Nor should there be in yours. You heard him confess and threaten to shoot me to keep his secret safe. You have done the women of the East End a service – a great service – Lord John. I only regret that you will receive no recognition for it.

LJR   A fellah don't expect a gong for shootin' a mad dog. Anyway, I think your secret's safe enough. That constable was sure that it was an accident.

MH   What is it that Ovid says: '*Bene qui latuit bene vixit, dominatur enim fraus in omnibus?*'

SH   You have the right poet but I think a more appropriate line would have been: '*Causa latet; vis est notissima.*' Curious that a volume dedicated to the gentle art of seduction should prove to contain so apt an epitaph for the generation's most savage killer.

LJR   It has been said that love and hatred are but separate barrels of the same shot-gun. If you gentlemen have no further need of my services tonight, I'll push on. I have a case of trade gin ridin' on the best of three frames at Cook's.

SH   Lord John, let me express my . . .

LJR   No need, Holmes. Fellah's got to do his duty; even if it ain't always pleasant or regular. You know where I am if you need me again.

MH   I really think you will be safer in the wilds of the Matto Grosso than if you were to remain as assistant to my brother for very much longer. I shall, nonetheless, inform the Duke

LJR   that you studiously avoided all trouble during your stay in town. If I do not see you before you sail, have a safe journey. Thank you. No, you needn't ring for a man; I can find my own way out.

MH   You were, I think, Sherlock, most fortunate to have a man like Roxton available when you needed him. You never intended to take Watson alive, of course; you required him dead so that there would be no chance that he would reveal his relationship with your room-mate. You had to engineer his escape from Baker Street; you would hardly want him dead there, would you?

SH   No, I could have tackled him with the jack-knife had that been my intention. Things seem to have turned out better than I had hoped; and certainly better than I deserved following the débâcle of the other morning. By the bye, you can tell your people in Yorkshire that Amelia will not be with them for very much longer. There is no reason now to keep her out of London. I shall have to go up and bring her back myself since that is what I told her I would do.

MH   What do you intend to do about the police authorities and the Whitechapel murderer? Only three people know the truth of what has occurred. Roxton, on whose discretion we may, I think, rely and ourselves.

SH   That is what I meant when I said that I had to talk to you of your part in the end of Jack the Ripper. I have already had some thoughts on the subject but I must give the matter some more consideration. I will be in touch with you in a day or so and we can discuss the matter more fully. As for the police, I think that, for the moment, we should say nothing to them. The police are public servants and, as with any servants, it is enough merely to pay their wages; it is not necessary to make them privy to your confidences as well.

CHAPTER 13

Correspondence

The narratives that we have followed until now have come to an end. This chapter contains the letters, telegrams, notes and memoranda that, in part at least, explain why and how those narratives came to be written. Each document is individually identified and its date – where known – is given.

The first document is a short letter from Conan Doyle dated the 21st of November and reads:

> Dear Mr Holmes,
>   I write at the urgent – not to say impassioned – insistence of my fellow practitioner who wishes me to convey to you his heartfelt gratitude for your visit earlier today. He wishes me to tell you how much he has benefited from the few minutes he was able to spend with you and he claims that your conversation has done him more good than my ministrations. (I am forced to admit that, as a physician, I have never seen such a marked change in a sufferer's condition brought about by nought more than the exchange of a dialogue of twenty minutes' duration.) Watson continues to improve; his pulse and heartbeat are both stronger and his periods of wakefulness are lengthening. It is still too soon to know when he might be allowed to set foot outside of his bed but I entertain hopes that this might be accomplished rather sooner than I had previously suggested to you and possibly by the weekend. I will be in contact in a day or two to inform you of when I think he will be able to receive visitors who may do more than hold his hand and talk to him.

You will, no doubt, be relieved to hear that Watson has so far made no mention of the case upon which the two of you were engaged when he came upon his wound. He speaks rather incoherently of you and of two ladies named Constance and Mary. The former was, I believe, his late wife; the latter I take to be his mother – though he speaks of her in the present. I am sure that these fancies will pass as the fever recedes.

Please be assured that I will write again in a day or two, or sooner if the need should arise.

Doyle

The second document is a note upon the stationery of the Diogenes Club, Pall Mall, and is dated the day following the preceding item. It reads:

Sherlock,

Following our discussions of yesterday evening, I wonder if you have yet had time to arrange your thoughts. It is absolutely imperative now that I have more facts as to your immediate plans. Since I doubt that either threat or bribe would induce you to dine two consecutive nights here perhaps I might prevail upon you to provide dinner – a cold collation ought not to tax your housekeeping unduly – and I will raid the cellars here for something suitable. I shall call at eight o'clock. If this should interfere with your plans I have allowed you sufficient time to rearrange your schedule.

Mycroft

It is fortunate for us that Sherlock Holmes was a methodical man. The carefully indexed scrapbooks of newspaper cuttings and the cross-referenced card index system of which Watson tells us are evidence of this methodology, and he was particularly thorough in his handling of the correspondence in the Ripper case. On the back of each letter or other message he received Holmes drafted his reply and then carefully noted the time, date and method of that reply's despatch.

Because of Holmes's thoroughness we know that he sent a note by means of the messenger service saying:

Dear Brother,

I shall be delighted to entertain you this evening and, since your visits to me are so rare as to be almost non-existent, I trust you will understand my desire to turn the evening into something of a celebration. I have some guinea fowl and an excellent ham which I am sure you will have no trouble complementing from the club's cellars. I also have a perfect Stilton and I suggest a bottle of the reserve port would not go amiss.

Despite the preparations I feel I should point out that it has been said that 'conversation makes the finest main course' and, if that is the case, I can promise you a veritable banquet tonight.

Sherlock

P.S. I suggest that you do not arrange for your coach to call too early. I have the feeling that you will be in celebratory mood and in no hurry to leave.

There is no record of what was said between the two brothers during their dinner.

Chronologically the next letter is one from Dr Watson. It is dated the 25th of November, and reads:

My dear Holmes,

I trust that you will forgive my invalid scrawl – have you ever tried to write a letter resting upon nothing more secure than a book perched upon your knees? – but I felt that I must write to let you know the effect that your visit here this afternoon has had upon me. It is too soon to say that I am recovered but it is not too soon to say that I am upon the road to recovery. I am aware that my pulse and temperature are almost back to normal. It is a poor physician who, left alone with his hunter and thermometer, cannot check upon these himself. I am also convinced that my colour and vigour are both improving.

Let me take the opportunity to thank you again for the books that you so kindly brought. The Clark Russell I have read but the Rider Haggard I have not, despite the fact that it is now some two years since it was published and from the first dozen or so pages it promises to be a worthy successor to his first. And thinking of successors to the first, Doyle suggests that I begin to get back into harness by chronicling another of your cases. I think that the affair of the Sholto brothers and the Agra treasure would be rather suitable, don't you? Of course I shall not choose this subject should you have some objection to my doing so. If you have, perhaps you could suggest some other case. You know that I have always considered that you displayed your talents to great effect in the matter of the disappearance of the unfortunate Mr Etherege. Perhaps this would be a more suitable case history for public presentation?

Anyway, enough of the future. Your visit today has cheered me immeasurably. Your conversation and your cigar – Doyle complained after you had gone that it was too soon for me to resume my old habits and has said that he will permit me the occasional cigar only if I promise to forgo the lure of alcohol and women – were welcome in equal part. Doyle has made a print of the photographic plate he exposed while you were here and I think you will agree that it cannot harm your work. Even your mother would have difficulty in recognising you from this picture. Doyle says it's something to do with the exposure; whatever that might be. I enclose a copy for you so that you may be assured that you are unlikely to be recognised as a result of this picture as you travel about. I am not altogether happy with the view it presents of me. I know that I am what may be termed solid but I think that the photographic process has tended to make me look a little more meaty than I am.

I must close now since I am beginning to feel a trifle fatigued and I want to give this to Doyle so that he may have Billy take it to the posting box. I thank you, old friend, for your kindness and would like you to know that I shall be available to assist you in your work just as soon as I may. I will write again in a day or two.

One who is proud to call himself,

Your friend,

Watson

There is a short note from Conan Doyle attached to this letter with a treasury tag expressing the following sentiment:

Dear Mr Holmes,

I regret that my preoccupation with another case did not allow me enough time to talk with you after you had seen Watson today. I am concerned about his preoccupation with his mother; and the fact that he appears to be confusing her with some lady by the name of Miss Morstan. This lady would appear to be either a figment of his imagination (since he seems to see her covered in fabulous pearls or endowed with some vast treasure) or a remembrance from his time in India (since he often links her name with those of somebody known as Khitmutger and with some sort of monster or demon known as Tonga). I do not believe that these delusions can be salubrious for him and would welcome any suggestions that you might have that would help me to eradicate them from his mind.

Doyle

Upon the reverse of this letter Holmes has written:

Wired Doyle morning of Monday 26th suggesting that he request Watson to give him the story of his meeting with Miss Morstan and the events involving the Sholto brothers and the Agra treasure ensuing therefrom. Indicated that he should regard wire as my blessing to reveal facts of case if Watson should feel obliged to keep my professional secrets. Also informed Doyle that Watson's mother had died when he was quite young and that I did not know if Watson held any memories of her.

146

The next letter carries the imprint of the crest of the Diogenes Club and is dated Wednesday the 28th of November 1888. It reads:

Sherlock,

You may have wondered why I have allowed a week to elapse before responding to your extraordinary suggestion although, being aware of the opinion that you have of me, I have no doubt that you ascribe the delay to what you see as my *languor*. How many times have I told you that speed and thoroughness are rarely compatible? However, I may say that I have now completed a total review of the course of action that you propose and feel that I must dissociate myself – and my department – from it. I foresee the following three major difficulties.

1. How can you hope to persuade the police authorities that you have unmasked the murderer if you are not prepared to give them a name? Whatever opinion you may hold of the official detective force it is my belief that they are largely dedicated and efficient officers. They will not cease in their own investigations simply upon the word of an enthusiastic amateur; however illustrious his reputation or his connexions might be.

2. Even supposing that you could concoct some story that would satisfy the police at present, could you be sure that the truth might not come out at a later date? This affair has caught the imagination of the public – and of the gutter press – in a manner that I do not believe you fully comprehend. Were you to consider the wider context for a moment you would realise that, if no satisfactory official solution to the mystery is ever offered, then sensationalist newspapermen might still be writing of it in ten years' time: perhaps longer. This might have two serious effects. It could undermine public confidence in the ability and integrity of the police force and it might result in some wholly innocent

person being named as the 'real' murderer. This last is entirely unacceptable.

3.   You have forgotten Watson. Although I have only met him twice and have not had an opportunity to talk to him very seriously, he seemed to me an alert and intelligent sort. How do you think you are going to persuade him to forget the events of an evening which must be indelibly engraved upon his mind? Do you, perhaps, hope to convince him that he fell asleep and discharged his own pistol through his leg? And remember, Watson expects to be taken into your fullest confidence; or so you have told me. Will he be content for you merely to say that you caught the man and there's an end of it? I think not.

In view of the foregoing I am sure that you will understand that I cannot allow myself, or any government body, to become involved in your proposed scheme. You may be sure that truth will out. The Dane has it that 'Foul deeds will rise, Though all the world o'erwhelm them'. I cannot support you, Sherlock; indeed, should you proceed, I must oppose you.

                                                            Mycroft

Sherlock Holmes lost no time in replying to this letter. Although his drafted response is not dated, the first sentence indicates when it was composed. It seems likely that it would have been sent fairly quickly. The reply reads:

Mycroft,

    Your letter of yesterday really does make things most difficult for me. Your indicated objections are not nearly so heavy as you imagine them.

    You ask how I can hope to satisfy the authorities that I have unmasked the murderer. *I* will not. *We* will. You may have been successful in fooling others as to your abilities and ambitions but I know who runs the department in which you work – and we both know that it is you. I am surprised that, although you have had a week in which to consider the questions, you appear not to have arrived at what I would have thought were the obvious solutions. However, I shall enumerate:

Firstly, you ask how we may convince the authorities that the murderer is dead without having to reveal his name. This is very simple. Officially we say nothing. Unofficially you let fall to one or two members of your club, if you can ever get to talk to them, that is, that the newspaper suggestions that the killer was a foreign *agent provocateur* were closer to the truth than the Government is willing to admit. The identity of the killer cannot be revealed because he was not acting with the blessing, or even the knowledge, of his own government. When they discovered the truth, they arranged to have the man disposed of quickly and quietly. This story will, I think, satisfy everybody. It will confirm the general prejudice that these ghastly crimes could not possibly be the work of an Englishman; those who believe themselves 'in the know' will cease puzzling over the killer's identity and will begin trying to deduce the identity of the country from which he hailed and whether or not that country's government really had no knowledge of what he was about; those persons, and particularly, those police officers, not 'in the know' will realise from the attitude of those who believe themselves to be that something has happened and will inevitably speculate amongst themselves as to what could have caused the higher authorities to say nothing. Their speculations can only be to our advantage since they will do naught more than 'muddy the water' and the muddier the water the more difficult it will be to see the fish.

Secondly, you ask how we can expect such a story to stand the test of the years. Would not such an obvious fabrication be found out? It probably would if anyone were to delve into the details of the case, but I doubt that anybody will. After all, these murders are obviously the work of a madman and the case lacks any real features of interest and has achieved its current position in the minds of the public only because of the unpleasantness of its details. But, against the remote chance of future scandal-mongers, we will prepare a second line of defence. As you begin one false trail I will begin another. I have already in my files the details of two men who would perfectly fit the role of decoy. One is a Polish Jew (which would tie in with the message scrawled upon the wall in Goulston Street) and the other is a Russian doctor (which would explain the murderer's medical knowledge). I believe, however, that our best course of action would be to keep a close watch on the inquest reports over the next few months. It is extremely unlikely that we will be lucky enough to find a perfect dupe but we might find some unfortunate man who believed himself – or who was believed by others – to be insane. Such a man could be made into a first-class 'suspect' in retrospect. And, remember, the longer it takes for this 'suspect's' name to become known the harder it will be for anybody to prove or disprove his guilt.

Thirdly, you suggest that I have forgotten Watson but you must be aware that my only concern at the moment is for Watson. I have already put in hand steps that I hope will lead Watson to believe that he is suffering from a relapse and that it is his old wound from Maiwand that now troubles him. This has happened before and there is every reason to believe that he will accept what he is told; especially since he has no reason to think that he is being deceived. If he recalls the face of his brother (which he glimpsed only briefly in the flame of his revolver) we shall merely tell him that this vision is a result, and not the cause, of his fever.

You will see, therefore, that I do not think there is any real reason why we should not be able to accomplish the things that I suggest we should attempt. I urge you, brother, to offer me your assistance in this matter. I have no wish to oppose you and feel that such opposition cannot be in the best interests of the country. I must also tell you that my plans are laid and that if you do not stand with me then you must stand against me. That fact may not cause you any particular concern but I would ask you to consider what would be the effect of the publication of the facts in the matters of the King of Scandinavia's dilemma or the outcome of my researches into the household misfortunes of the Dutch ruling family. I mention these so that you will recall that there are other cases, some rather nearer to home, that I could also make public should the need arise. You will know that my loyalty to my country is such that I would not take such a course of action unless it were absolutely necessary; to distract the radical press from some other topic, perhaps.

I am sure that you now see that it will not only be my – and Watson's – interest that you serve if you aid me but the country's also. I look forward to your reply; and your cooperation.

Your dutiful brother,
Sherlock

The only response to this letter is a note from Mycroft Holmes dated Saturday, the 1st of December, which reads:

Expect me at five o'clock this evening and ensure that we will not be disturbed.

M.

Holmes also received a letter with the same date as the above memorandum. The letter is from Watson:

My Dear Holmes,

I cannot even begin to tell you how much better I feel today. I shall shortly be back in Town; of that you may be certain. You will never guess what has happened to bring about this change in me. I have had a visit from Miss Morstan, who, apparently, was visiting a relative in the town and happened to run into young Billy. Where are your fine theories as to the rarity of coincidence now? Do you think it could be fate at work on my behalf? I must say Miss Morstan looks wonderfully well – one would never guess at the great strain she has so recently endured. She makes me feel quite the counterfeit, lying here and pretending to be unwell. I have secured her promise that she will accompany me to the theatre, bringing Mrs Forrester, naturally. Do you know of something that is playing and would be suitable?

As to my own case – I continue to improve with each passing day. My bouts of sleep and wakefulness are now completely normal; my appetite has returned and Doyle has allowed me out of bed for a few short periods. Walking pains me somewhat and I tire rather quickly but aside from these problems I really am most well.

I may write again but I hope from the bottom of my heart that the next communication that you hear from me will be the sound of my foot upon the stairs in Baker Street.

    Yours,
    Watson

The next document is a postcard bearing an address in Lower Camberwell. It is brief and beautifully penned. It is dated the 3rd of December.

Dear Mr Holmes,

    Your stratagem worked like a charm. Billy met me at the station and escorted me to Dr Doyle's house. Dr Watson seemed quite pleased to see me and I hope that I was able to cheer him up a little. He stated that it was his firm intention to return to London in the very near future and, consequently, I did not offer to visit him again. I did, however, agree to go to the theatre with him when this should be convenient. I rather imagine that you will know the details of this visit before I do since no doubt Dr Watson will discuss with you the suitability of several plays before making the

arrangements. If I may be of any further assistance to
yourself or Dr Watson please do not hesitate to contact
me: you know where I may be reached.
    Yours sincerely,
    Mary Morstan (Miss)

Upon the bottom of this card Holmes has scrawled 'On ne
badine avec l'amour'.
    Dated the day following the above postcard is a memo-
randum from Mycroft Holmes, again written upon the
stationery of the Diogenes Club.

Sherlock,
    Have you not told me that Watson keeps a journal
or diary? Will not this volume contain full details of your
investigations into the Whitechapel outrages? How will
you overcome this problem? Even the good doctor's
suspicions must be aroused were the book to disappear.
He has told me that, as you, he has a horror of throwing
away any document connected with one of your cases.
Something to do with his literary ambitions, no doubt.
                                    M.

Holmes answered his brother's queries on the 5th of
December. The draft for this note reads:

Dear Brother,
    Not unusually, you are about a fortnight late. I had
come to the conclusion that I would have to rearrange
the immediate past for Watson's benefit at the time when
I first broached my intentions to you. In order to do this
I have rewritten Watson's diary. This was not as difficult
as you might suppose.
    Watson does not write daily in his journal; rather he
keeps a mass of rough notes and jottings which he writes
up when the going is slack. He has not had much time
for writing recently. The hectic business of the Agra
treasure was followed in a very few days by our

involvement with Sir Henry Baskerville and our prolonged visit to Devonshire. Upon the day following our return from Baskerville Hall we were involved in the hunt for the Whitechapel murderer. Consequently Watson's notes are in considerable disarray. I have reworked some of his sheets to fit the pattern that I have already outlined to you.

I believe I may say that I have thought of everything.

Your dutiful, but increasingly impatient, brother,
Sherlock

Mycroft Holmes replied to his brother on the 7th of December in a short memorandum:

Sherlock,

I agree to assist you in your scheme subject to two provisos.

First. You speak in one of your letters of the possibility of finding a recently deceased man whom you can accuse. You must find a candidate acceptable to me before you proceed and you must see that this candidate's name somehow comes to the attention of the authorities in such a way that they believe he was the murderer but will not say so because they are unable to prove it. How will you achieve this?

Second. You must furnish me with all the facts of the case. The truth, I mean. I will arrange that these facts eventually come to light. This will not happen until we are all dead and long gone. You would perhaps be surprised to learn of some of the bundles of documents that are held in obscure corners of various Government departments. (I have recently, for example, read a truly remarkable letter from a lady which provides an explanation for the Little Corporal's lethargy on the morning of 18th June 1815 which seems never to have suggested itself to Creasy.) I believe that the truth must be told in the end. Although we may temporarily tamper

with it none of us has the moral right to permanently
alter or falsify history.

Mycroft

On Monday, the 10th of December, Holmes received a wire
from Southsea. The message is short and jubilant:

> I have secured my release from Doyle. Billy and I will
> be home this evening. I will not be fatigued and would
> be greatly pleased if you would make a booking for dinner.
> My club would be suitable.
>
> Watson

Holmes has written a brief note on the back of the telegram.
'Watson's club would not be suitable. Mrs Hudson and I will
rise to the occasion. Miss Morstan will be all the fare Watson
will need. Mrs Forrester must come and Roxton will make up
the number (if he has not yet sailed). A celebration here will
be apt and less taxing for the old campaigner. Beef, Baune,
fowl, pâté, gâteau, fruit. Mycroft's port.'

The next document is a letter written on Holmes's own
stationery dated the 12th of December which reads:

> Mr Holmes,
> You may recall that we had dealings together some three
> years ago in the matter of Mrs Comber of Margate. I
> should very much like to consult you in connection with
> a personal matter concerning my brother, Montague John
> Druitt.
> I learned yesterday that Montague has been missing
> from his chambers (he is a barrister) for more than a
> week and I immediately came up to town to make
> inquiries. His clerk is unable to offer any suggestion as
> to his whereabouts and Mr Valentine (who runs a school
> in Blackheath at which Montague taught until recently)
> also has no idea of what may have occurred. I have,
> however, learned that there has been some trouble but
> I would prefer to discuss these things with you rather
> than commit them to paper.

155

If it is convenient for you I shall call upon you at ten o'clock tomorrow morning. If this should conflict with plans you have already made, I may be reached at Horrex's, at the corner of Norfolk Street.

Wm. Druitt

P.S. Please forgive the appropriation of your notepaper but I came to town in such haste that I forgot to bring any of my own.

The short note written above is the last written in 1888. There are only two documents to come; both are dated in January 1889. The first is from Holmes to his brother and is dated the 5th.

Mycroft,

I shall be pleased to accept your invitation to dinner tomorrow. You may be sure that I shall let no case intrude upon my time between now and then and I look to you to ensure that no incident of national importance occurs to interfere with your own attendance. I enclose herewith for your perusal a clipping from today's *Southern Guardian*. Please look out any information you might have concerning the family in question. I shall have much to say to you touching them.

As you have insisted upon compiling a complete record of my activities in connexion with this matter I also enclose herewith a resumé of the notes I made during the night of the 8th/9th November last. I trust you will find these adequate.

Until tomorrow,
Sherlock

The last item is a final memorandum from Mycroft Holmes; it is dated the 7th of January and reads:

My dear Sherlock,

You have convinced me. I think that this unfortunate

young man, Druitt, will suit us admirably. You are sure
that his own family thought that he might have been
the murderer because of the madness that had already
manifested itself in his mother and because of his known
sexual proclivities. Watson was with you when you
received this information. You are convinced that Watson
will not be able to resist telling somebody that he knows
the identify of the criminal and so the false trail will be
laid. We must find the right person for Watson to confide
in but this ought not to be too difficult. A discreet but
confident individual who is not likely to blaze the
information abroad but is likely to confide in his family
or his diary. If we could select a suitable police official
of senior rank this would answer our needs perfectly.

I have now had the chance to read Watson's narrative,
as set down in his journal, which seems to me
commendable if somewhat lurid. I see that you have
already managed to incorporate a reference to Druitt into
the diary together with the suggestion that, though you
had grounds for suspicion, his suicide has robbed you
of the opportunity to catch him red-handed. Nicely done,
Sherlock. It is convincing; at least, I believe it will
convince Watson. Your statement of the parts of the story
in which Watson was not involved will ensure that
posterity may have the whole truth. I see that you have
chosen to adopt Watson's style for your parts of the
chronicle, which I think is a good idea. No one will ever
believe that you wrote it – at least no one who has read
one of your monographs. What is it that Pope says?

Such laboured nothings, in so strange a style
Amaze th'unlearn'd, and make the learned smile.

Let me again wish you all felicitations for your birthday
and permit me to express the hope that the run of success
which you have enjoyed since that extraordinary affair
of the disappearing egg continues; as long as it does we
need not concern ourselves with the expense of a police

college. You effect their training by example.
    With my very best wishes,
    Mycroft

P.S. I do not profess to be an authority where *affaires de coeur* are concerned but I would not be at all surprised if you were soon to lose Watson to Miss Morstan; his visage as he left last night to meet the lady at the theatre was that of a man who has resolved upon his destiny and rushes happily to embrace it. As it were. M.

CHAPTER 14

A Retrospection

Now that we have come to the end of this extraordinary story we must ask whether it has any basis in fact. Much has been written about both Sherlock Holmes and Jack the Ripper and if we recapitulate the main events of this narrative and compare them with what has already been published, how will they stand up?

The story begins on Saturday, the 20th of October 1888. Holmes and Watson have returned to London (the previous day) at the completion of the case of the Hound of the Baskervilles. On the Saturday they are visited by Major Smith who is the Commissioner of the City police force and who brings with him a human kidney and a letter received by George Lusk of the Whitechapel Vigilance Committee. Major Smith asks Holmes to help and Holmes agrees to try but states that he does not think he will be able to be of much assistance. During the afternoon Holmes and Watson visit the sites of the two murders committed on the night of the 30th of September.

Firstly, the 20th of October 1888 *was* a Saturday. Indeed, wherever the dates quoted can be checked against alternative authorities such as newspapers or the previously published books dealing with the Ripper case, they are found to be correct. The dating of the various cases that Watson has chronicled is a far more complicated matter, however. It has been the theme of a number of books and is too vast a subject to be discussed here. Suffice it to say – as Michael and Mollie Hardwick do in *The Sherlock Holmes Companion* (John Murray 1962) – 'We cannot entirely rely on Watson's dating of the stories which he has recorded: his facts we do not question too closely, but his chronology is undoubtedly rocky. Other commentators have analysed fully the extraordinary contradictions in date which beset the seeker after Watsonian truth. It is all of a piece with his remarkable vagueness on other matters.' Michael Harrison in *The World of Sherlock Holmes* (Frederick Muller 1973) comments: 'Now, we know that Watson, not only in the interests of "tact", to say nothing of the avoidance of expensive libel actions, but mostly because his professional training had conditioned him to discretion, always made some alteration, great or small, in the names of the *dramatis personae*, in the locations of the adventures and even the dates involved.' I have taken as my guide through this minefield the late W. S. Baring-Gould who printed his *The Chronological Holmes* privately in 1955 and incorporated that chronology into his *Sherlock Holmes of Baker Street, A Life of the World's First Consulting Detective* which was published in 1962 by Rupert Hart Davis. Baring-Gould dates the Baskerville case to 1888; from the 25th of September to the 20th October. Major Henry Smith was the Commissioner of the City of London Police (he was actually the Assistant Commissioner, but the Commissioner, Sir James Fraser, was on sick leave at this time) and he seems to have been the sort of man who would consult Holmes in the sort of circumstances he found himself in. As with the dates, the people referred to are always correctly named and identified (e.g.: Henry Matthews *was* the Home Secretary; Sir James Whitehead *was* the incoming Lord Mayor of London, etc.). The letter and postcard signed Jack the Ripper are both authentic and reproductions of them and of the Metropolitan Police poster can be found in *The Complete Jack the Ripper* by Donald Rumbelow (the W. H. Allen 1975 edition). The letter 'from hell' *was* received by Mr Lusk (who *was* a founder member of the Whitechapel Vigilance Committee) on the 15th of October and a facsimile of it and of the writing on the wall can be found in *Jack the Ripper: The Final Solution* by Stephen Knight (George G. Harrap 1976). There is no independent evidence that Holmes and Watson visited the murder sites.

A Retrospection

Holmes spends Sunday, the 21st of October, searching his files for suspects and comes up with two: Ostrog and Kosminski. We know that Sherlock Holmes kept a card index as part of his records ('The Five Orange Pips') but we have no knowledge as to the information that it contained. These two suspects become more interesting later.

On the 22nd of October Holmes and Watson visit Inspector Gregson at Scotland Yard to try to find out the details of the previous Ripper murders but are interrupted and thrown out by Sir Charles Warren. Holmes refuses to help the Metropolitan Police until Warren is replaced but later tells Major Smith that he will give whatever help he can to the City force.

There is no evidence that this visit ever took place. Inspector Gregson is real enough (he is working with Inspector Lestrade in *A Study in Scarlet*) and Sir Charles Warren was the Commissioner for the Metropolitan Police and had been since early 1886. Warren appears to have been universally disliked and he has been accused by writers on the Ripper case of everything from incompetence to active participation in an official cover-up. It might be useful to ignore the speculation and look to see if there is any evidence to suggest Warren's attitude to his role as Metropolitan Police Commissioner. Warren's predecessor, Sir Edmund Henderson, was forced to resign following the £50,000 worth of damage caused by a crowd of 2,000 rioters on what was to become known as 'Black Monday' – the 8th of February 1886. It is not difficult to imagine what Warren's instructions must have been when he was appointed. He was to prevent a recurrence at all costs. He quickly reorganised the Metropolitan Police along military lines and kept the peace by the simple threat of meeting violence with violence. Warren's attitude to policework is clearly shown in the constitution of the 'top brass' at Scotland Yard; when Warren took over this comprised one soldier, two lawyers, one detective and two policemen but by the time he resigned it was six soldiers, one lawyer and one policeman. It was inevitable that sooner or later Warren's challenge would be taken up.

The confrontation came on 'Bloody Sunday' – the 13th of November 1887. Warren had banned all meetings from Trafalgar Square, but a rally was announced. Something like 100,000 unemployed converged on the square to listen to speakers like Annie Besant, Eleanor Marx, George Bernard Shaw and William Morris. Warren's instructions read like a battle plan (they can be found in full in *The Ripper File* by Elwyn Jones and John Lloyd – Weidenfeld and Nicolson 1975) and include the disposition of 300 Life Guards and 300 Grenadier Guards who 'If called upon . . . will line the parapet with fixed bayonets'. The day ended with more than 150 people requiring hospital treatment and Warren triumphant.

In his book *The Story of Scotland Yard* (Arthur Barker 1965) Sir Robert Howe, a former head of the CID, describes Warren as 'an imperious, bad-tempered man who not only forfeited the co-operation of his officers but was in constant disagreement with the Home Office. As far as possible he ignored the CID.' With this background in mind Warren's attitude to Holmes, who was not only a detective but a private detective, is seen to be in character. The details of this visit, then, though not independently corroborated, seem reasonable.

There is a gap in the narrative from the 22nd of October to the 8th of November during which Holmes was engaged upon the cases of Colonel Upwood and the Nonpareil Club and Madame Montpensier. Baring-Gould dates these cases to 'between Sat., 20 Oct. and late Nov. 1888' which, if not exact, is very close.

On the 8th of November Inspector Abberline visits Holmes and asks him to reconsider his decision not to help the Metropolitan Police. Abberline also explains to Holmes why he believes that the Ripper is likely to strike again soon. Inspector Fred Abberline was one of the officers in charge of the Ripper investigations. Sir Melville Macnaughten (who went to Scotland Yard as Chief Constable in 1889 and retired as Assistant Commissioner of Police and Chief of the Criminal Investigation Department in 1913) says of Abberline, 'He knew the East End of London as few men have since known it' (*Days*

A Retrospection

of My Years by Sir Melville Macnaughten – Edward Arnold 1914). He appears to have been a conscientious officer and his reports (which are quoted extensively by Stephen Knight) show him to be capable and comprehensive in his work. The conditions that he describes as prevailing in Whitechapel ring true: the pattern of panic followed by trepidation followed by a feeling that perhaps 'this time' the Ripper had had his day. It is also certainly true that the preparations for the procession of the Lord Mayor elect (Sir James Whitehead) were detailed and elaborate. The incoming Lord Mayor wished to exclude the 'circus element' from that year's procession, but when the news of the Ripper's last murder broke during the day the crowd went wild and the Lord Mayor's Show turned into a near-riot.

When Inspector Abberline sees that he has not been able to persuade Holmes to help him, he delivers a summons from Mycroft, Sherlock's brother. In an interview, Mycroft tells Holmes that the Queen herself has asked that he, Sherlock, involve himself in the case. Is this turn of events likely? It is by no means unlikely. Mycroft Holmes's own official position is unclear but Watson quotes Sherlock Holmes as saying of his elder brother (in 'The Adventure of the Bruce-Partington Plans'), 'you would also be right in a sense if you said that occasionally he *is* the British Government'. Mycroft was certainly in a position to be entrusted with the Palace's errands and it is quite likely that he would have been the man charged with getting Holmes involved in the case, even if the two had not been brothers. Would Queen Victoria have wished Holmes to take a hand in the investigation? Probably. She was deeply interested in the details of the Ripper case and had no high opinion of the police force. Dan Farson records that she rebuked the Home Secretary as follows: 'The Queen fears that the detective department is not so efficient as it might be.' Later, after the murder of Mary Kelly, she sent a telegram to the Prime Minister saying, 'This new most ghastly murder shows the absolute necessity for some dedicated action. All these courts must be lit, and our detectives improved.' And,

163

Her Majesty had already met Holmes in circumstances that would have given her a tremendous impression of his powers. In October 1879 Holmes, in the case that Watson has called 'The Musgrave Ritual', recovered 'nothing less than the ancient crown of the kings of England'. Of the aftermath of the case Michael Harrison, in his book *The World of Sherlock Holmes*, says, 'certain it is that the restored Regalia were not rendered up to their rightful Owner without her having graciously commanded the presence of the two young men (Reginald Musgrave and Sherlock Holmes) who had been instrumental in bringing back from supposed oblivion treasures of such worth. This private audience of Her Majesty to which Holmes was commanded in the October of 1879 was almost certainly his first meeting with his Sovereign. There were to be many more such audiences before her death, twenty-two years later.'

Holmes's next move is to disguise himself as a prostitute and visit Whitechapel in the hope that he might pick up some sort of a lead from the other women of the streets. In the course of his enquiries Holmes meets Mary Jane Kelly who had been in service to Watson during the time that the good doctor had deserted Baker Street and set up in his own establishment with his first wife, Constance. Holmes arranges to call upon Mary Jane early the following morning to see if she has been able to find out anything. When Holmes arrives at Number 13 Miller's Court he finds that Mary Jane is dead – murdered and horribly mutilated by the Ripper. Holmes examines the body and then goes to leave when he discovers that he has smeared blood down the front of the blouse he is wearing. He takes Mary's shawl and puts it around his shoulders to conceal the bloodstains. As he tries to leave Miller's Court he is mistaken for her by a woman who speaks to him.

Holmes's skill with make-up and his *penchant* for adopting disguises are legendary. I think that there is only one occasion when Holmes disguises himself as a woman recorded in the published cases (in 'The Mazarin Stone'), but that disguise was so effective that Billy confessed that Holmes 'Fairly took me in,

he did, and I ought to know his ways by now'. Since Baring-
Gould dates this case to the summer of 1903 Billy certainly
should have known Holmes's ways by then and it perhaps
explains why Holmes disguises himself as an old woman and
not, as he had done fourteen years previously, as a 24-year-old.

Mary Jane Kelly was the fifth and last victim of Jack the
Ripper. She was born in Limerick but was taken to
Carmarthenshire when she was still a child. Joseph Barnet
(with whom Mary Jane was living until a few days prior to her
death), who gave evidence at her inquest, said that Mary Jane
claimed that she had been to France and that on her return to
England 'she had lived in a fashionable house in the West End
for a while'. It must be pointed out that Mary Kelly appears
to have had a highly developed sense of the dramatic and too
much credence should not be placed upon her statements.
However, having said that, is there any evidence that she was
employed by Watson? Yes, there is. In the record Watson has
given us of the case he called 'A Scandal in Bohemia' he tells
us that Holmes was able to deduce that he had 'a most clumsy
and careless servant girl'. Watson responds, 'As to Mary Jane,
she is incorrigible, and my wife has given her notice'. Baring-
Gould states that Watson married Miss Constance Adams of
San Francisco on the 1st of November 1886 and goes on to say:
'Shortly thereafter he purchased a small practice in
Kensington.' This is by no means conclusive but it does show
that it is at least possible that Mary Jane Kelly was in Watson's
employ for a period when he was living in Kensington which
could be the basis for her statement that 'she lived . . . in the
West End for a while'.

There is no independent evidence that Holmes ever visited
Miller's Court. His description of it and of the inside of
Number 13, however, are perfectly accurate. (A description
of Miller's Court appears in *The Ripper File* and a photograph
of the court appears in *The Complete Jack the Ripper*.)

Holmes claims that he was accosted by a woman as he was
leaving Miller's Court, and this statement provides the solution
to a mystery that has persisted since the inquest on Mary Kelly.

At the inquest one witness, Mrs Caroline Maxwell, claimed to have seen her standing at the corner of the entry to the court 'on Friday morning, from eight to half past eight'. Mrs Maxwell claimed this despite the fact that the coroner had told her, 'You must be very careful in your evidence because it is different to other people's.' Mrs Maxwell has had a bad press from all the writers on the Ripper case. 'The woman was lying, or it was a case of mistaken identity' (Donald McCormick in *The Identity of Jack the Ripper* – Jarrolds 1959). 'She had obviously got the wrong day' (*The Ripper File*). 'Whether Mrs Maxwell was lying, mistaken or drunk has never been explained. The only certainty is that she was wrong' (*Jack the Ripper: The Final Solution*). The story told in this narrative is the only one that will satisfy the facts. Dr Thomas Bond performed the post-mortem on Mary Kelly and his report dated the 10th of November 1888 is printed in full in *The Complete Jack the Ripper*. It says in part: 'one or two o'clock in the morning would be the probable time of the murder'. Stephen Knight records that Mrs Maxwell's statement was taken by Inspector Abberline himself *on the morning of the murder* (since the body was not discovered until 10.45 a.m., Abberline must have been quick off the mark). Since her statement was taken on the same day that she claimed to have seen Mary Kelly, it is unlikely that Mrs Maxwell could have been confused about the date. There is no suggestion that she was either lying or drunk; had she been drunk when she made her statement the police would not have called her to the inquest and had she been lying it is probable that she would have made up a more sensational tale than that she talked to the victim. She would probably have spoken of seeing the murderer at least. But she didn't. She made her statement (that she had seen and talked to Mary Kelly between eight and eight-thirty on the morning of the 9th of November – when Dr Bond reckoned that the victim had been dead for between six and seven and a half hours) on the morning of the discovery of the murder and she stuck to it, despite the efforts of the police and coroner to get her to change her story. She must have believed her story and if she could not have seen Kelly then she must have seen somebody who looked like Kelly. She must have seen Sherlock Holmes.

At this time it is probably not possible to prove or disprove Mrs Maxwell's statements, but it is worth saying that the solution offered by the narrative published here does at least provide a reasonable explanation for an otherwise inexplicable contradiction.

The next major incident in the narrative occurs when Holmes returns to Baker Street and is confronted by Abberline and the young constable who accuses Dr Watson of being Jack the Ripper. The constable is not identified but is obviously P. C. Spicer. P. C. Spicer did exist and he has recorded the details of his arrest of 'the Ripper' in a letter that he sent to the *Daily Express*. The letter was published on Monday, the 16th of March 1931 (sandwiched between an item headed 'Shades of Old London' which detailed how the face of the capital was changing and includes this comment: 'Upper Baker Street, again, has grown up from quiet houses into mammoth flats. Sherlock Holmes, who had his rooms in Upper Baker Street, should he revisit his old haunts to-day, would need the best of his detective ability to find out where he lived' and an item headed 'Meet Miss 1931 – In Wax' which sets out 'what the 1931 Summer Girl will look like') and is the subject of an article headed 'I caught Jack the Ripper'. The letter writer is named as 'Mr Robert Clifford Spicer, of Saville-row, Woodford Green, Essex, who was a uniformed constable, aged twenty-two, at the time the Jack the Ripper outrages were terrorising London'. The story given in the letter is substantially the same as that told in the narrative. This letter is well known and is quoted in many of the books dealing with the Ripper. Mr Spicer's account is usually discounted because the incident is normally dated to the night of the double murder (the 30th of September) and the event took place at 'a quarter to two in the morning'. The arguments are that the Ripper is known to have killed twice that night and the suggestion that he would have attempted a third murder the same night is discounted by several authors without even pointing out that the Mitre Square murder is officially timed to between 1.30 a.m. and 1.45 a.m., which effectively places Jack the Ripper in two places at the same moment. However, Mr Spicer does not give a date in his letter. His comment is: 'I had the pleasure of capturing him, and taking him to Commercial-street police station, after he had committed two murders.' What does this mean? We have no way of knowing how many murders Mr Spicer reckoned that the Ripper committed. Richard Whittington-Egan in his book *A Casebook on Jack the Ripper* (Wildy and Sons 1975) states: 'What is not, perhaps, generally realised, is that it was in the reports following the murder of Chapman that, for the first time, the murders of Emma Smith, Martha Turner, Mary Ann Nichols and Annie Chapman were linked, so that Chapman, actually, as we now believe, the Ripper's second victim, was at that time counted as his fourth.' Martha Turner (or Tabram) was killed on the 7th of August 1888. Mary Ann Nichols was killed on the 31st of August. It seems likely, therefore, that Mr Spicer's arrest would have occurred sometime between these dates. This ties in perfectly with the statement attributed to P. C. Spicer in this manuscript that the date of the incident was 'about the middle of August'. Spicer states that Watson looks a lot like the Ripper. In the *Daily Express* letter Mr Spicer gives the following description of the man he arrested: 'He was always dressed the same [remember, Spicer claimed to have seen the man several times after the arrest] – high hat, black suit with silk facings, and a gold watch and chain. He was about 5 feet 8 or 9 inches and about 12 stone, fair moustache, high forehead, and rosy cheeks'. Is there any other evidence that this is a description of Jack the Ripper? Possibly. There was a witness who came forward to say that he had seen one of the victims with a man who may have been the murderer. George Hutchinson knew Mary Kelly – and knew her well enough for her to try to borrow sixpence from him. Hutchinson was not able to give evidence at the inquest on Mary Kelly but he went to the Commercial Street police station at six o'clock on the day of the inquest (the 12th of November) to make a statement. The statement explained that Hutchinson had seen Mary Kelly at the corner of Thrawl Street and Flower & Dean Street at 'about 1 a.m. 9th'. This puts Kelly with a man just a few minutes' walk from her room in Miller's Court (which was just off Dorset Street) at about the time when she was supposed to have been murdered. Dr Thomas Bond, who was a lecturer on forensic medicine and consulting surgeon to 'A' division and to the Great Western Railway, performed the post-mortem on Mary Kelly and, as has been noted above, put the time of death at 'one or two in the morning'. It seems very likely, then, that the man Hutchinson saw with Kelly was the murderer. Hutchinson's description of the man is quoted in full by Stephen Knight (who also reproduces a page of the statement). It reads: 'age about 34 or 35, height 5ft.6, complexion pale. Dark eyes and lashes. Slight moustache curled up each end and hair dark. Very surley [sic] looking. Dress, long dark coat, collar and cuffs trimmed astrakhan and a dark jacket under, light waistcoat, dark trousers, dark felt hat turned down in the middle, button boots and gaiters with white buttons, wore a very thick gold chain with linen collar, black tie with horse shoe pin, respectable appearance, walked very sharp. Jewish appearance. Can be identified.'

At first glance it may seem that the two descriptions are not very similar but, if one considers the image that each description suggests, I think that they are quite close. The richness of the dress is emphasised in both descriptions ('high hat, black suit with silk facings' and 'collar and cuffs trimmed astrakhan'), the height – for what it is worth – is similar ('5 feet 8 or 9 inches' and '5 ft 6') and, most important, the watch chain ('a gold watch and chain' and 'a very thick gold chain'). The narrative tells us that the man that Spicer saw greatly resembled Dr Watson. So, what did Dr Watson look like? We have, unfortunately, only two descriptions of him. One comes during the case of the blackmailer Charles Augustus Milverton, which is dated by Baring-Gould to January of 1899, and is presented by Inspector Lestrade who is unaware that the two masked men he is describing are, in fact, Holmes and Watson themselves. He says, 'The first fellow was a bit too active, but the second was caught by the under-gardener, and only got away after a struggle. He was a middle-sized, strongly-built man – square jaw, thick neck, moustache, a mask over his eyes.' Holmes is not impressed. 'That's rather vague,' he says. 'Why, it might even be a description of Watson.' 'It's true,' says the Inspector ('with much amusement'). 'It might be a description of Watson.' The other description of Watson occurs in the story 'His Last Bow' which takes place on the eve of the First World War. Watson is merely described as 'a heavily built, elderly man, with a grey moustache'. Since this was in 1914, when Watson would have been 62, it is reasonable to describe him as 'elderly' but, in 1888, he would have been in his mid-thirties, 36 to be precise, if we accept Baring-Gould's dating.

This brief résumé of the two most detailed descriptions of Jack the Ripper that are available and the only two descriptions of Dr Watson extant cannot be anything but inconclusive. All I would point out at this stage is that there is nothing in them which would mean that they could not be descriptions of the same man – or of two brothers who greatly resembled one another.

Holmes now decides that it is time for him to go on the offensive and, to this end, he asks Watson to select a woman from amongst his patients to act as a lure. Watson recommends a woman by the name of Amelia Palmer. Holmes is delighted to discover that Mrs Palmer knew one of the murdered women, Annie Chapman, and had actually given evidence at her inquest. Amelia (or Annie) Palmer (or Farmer) certainly did exist and her evidence to the Chapman inquest is quoted in several of the books on the Ripper. There is no indication that she knew either Holmes or Watson or that she was ever Watson's patient whether at the London or elsewhere.

Neither Watson's visit to Number 19, George Street, Whitechapel, nor Holmes's temporary employment as assistant to the keeper of that establishment, are confirmed elsewhere. The conditions that existed within the lodging-house might be thought to be exaggerated or sensationalised, but they are not.

Some of the conditions described by George R. Sims (*How the Poor Live*) and Andrew Mearns (*The Bitter Cry of Outcast London*), both of which were written in the 1880s, are far worse than those described by Watson.

The next major incident to occur in the narrative is the most spectacular in the whole story: the entrapment and the escape of the Ripper. Holmes follows Amelia and the murderer back to her room and, after checking that Watson is installed in the yard, confronts the pair. Jack escapes into the yard, wounds Watson and makes his getaway. Holmes takes steps to have Watson transported to safety and arranges for Amelia to be taken into protective custody. As has already been said, Amelia Palmer is real enough. Is there any evidence that she was ever attacked in the way this narrative details? There is, and it comes from the columns of *The Times* itself. In the issue for the 22nd of November 1888 there is a report that a woman named Annie Farmer was attacked in a room in a common lodging-house at Number 19, George Street. (Donald Rumbelow quotes the report in detail in *The Complete Jack the Ripper*.) The report states that Amelia was taken to a police station. (Mr Rumbelow anticipates this narrative by suspecting – his word – that 'this woman was the same Amelia Palmer who had been Annie Chapman's friend and was one of the last people to see her alive'.) A brief second report appeared in the paper next day. It has been suggested that the reports indicate that Amelia had been engaged in some sort of extortion or petty thievery but the evidence seems, to me, very inconclusive. Amelia apparently stated that she had met her assailant some twelve months earlier, 'and owing to this fact the officers are doubtful whether the man had anything to do with the murders'. Holmes's poor opinion of the reasoning powers of the police is amply confirmed.

Probably the most intriguing question raised by the whole narrative is that of Watson's wound. Watson gives a detailed and gruelling account of the wound that invalided him out of the army. He tells us in *A Study in Scarlet* that during the Battle of Maiwand (which Donald Featherstone dates to 27th of July

1880 in his *Colonial Small Wars* – David & Charles, 1973 – as well as providing a sketch map of the battle itself) he was 'struck on the shoulder by a Jezail bullet, which shattered the bone and grazed the subclavian artery'. This would seem definite and precise enough, but Watson tells us during the events of *The Sign of Four* which Baring-Gould dates to 1888 that he sprang from his chair and 'limped impatiently' about the room. Again, in the story of *The Noble Bachelor*, dated to October 1886 by Baring-Gould, Watson says that he had remained indoors all day because it was raining 'and the Jezail bullet which I brought back in one of my limbs as a relic of my Afghan campaign, throbbed with dull persistency'. Clearly some confusion exists here. Michael and Mollie Hardwick in *The Sherlock Holmes Companion*, alluding to this confusion say: 'Where, in fact, was the bullet-wound which pained him on the damp and windy days? It is very puzzling. We are forced to conclude that Watson received *two* (or more) bullets during the Afghan campaign, and, brave man that he was, thought one of them not worth chronicling at the time.' So, is there any other evidence to suggest that the leg wound Watson received at Maiwand was not as serious as his shoulder wound? I think there is. In *The Hound of the Baskervilles* which Baring-Gould dates to September and October of 1888 Watson states, 'I am reckoned fleet of foot' and recounts how he, Holmes and Lestrade see the Hound about to attack Sir Henry Baskerville. 'Never have I seen a man run as Holmes ran that night,' says Watson. 'He outpaced me as I outpaced the little professional.' Lestrade is described as 'lean and ferret-like' (*A Study in Scarlet*) and even though Lestrade speaks of his 'twenty years' experience' he is still described as 'a small, wiry bulldog of a man' who had 'sprung' from a first-class carriage during the Baskerville case. It is obvious, then, that Watson would have had to be running at a fair speed to outpace Lestrade in the way he tell us he did. This strongly suggests that at that time – October 1888 – Watson had no serious wound in his leg.

So, if we accept that Watson was wounded in the thigh as described in this narrative, is there any indication of how serious that wound might have been? Baring-Gould lists only one case taken by Holmes between 'late Nov. 1888 and Fri., 5 April – Sat., 20 April 1889'. One case in a period of approximately five months. This compares with twelve cases between the end of May and late November 1888 which is also approximately five months. This suggests either that Holmes's case load diminished rapidly or that Watson was unwilling or *unable* to accompany Holmes on his cases at this time. This would fit in with the serious wound described in this narrative. This explanation for Watson's apparent confusion over his wound resolves all of the various problems without introducing any of its own.

Let us stay with Watson for a little longer and consider two further points that crop up later in the narrative: the identification of Jack the Ripper as Henry Watson and the relationship between John Watson and Miss Mary Morstan in October and November 1888. Firstly, Henry Watson.

In *The Sign of Four* Holmes makes certain deductions from a watch that Watson says 'has recently come into my possession'. Holmes says that the watch belonged to Watson's elder brother, whose initials could have been H. W., and who had inherited it from his father. Watson's brother 'was a man of untidy habits – very untidy and careless. He was left with good prospects, but he threw away his chances, lived for some time in poverty with occasional short intervals of prosperity, and, finally, taking to drink, he died.' Watson confirms the accuracy of Holmes's deductions by stating that they are so accurate that Holmes must have made enquiries into the history of his 'unhappy brother'. Holmes protests that he never even knew that Watson had had a brother but had gleaned all his facts from the watch. All this took place in the middle of September 1888, according to Baring-Gould's dating. If we accept that Henry Watson did not die until the 21st of November, however, we must look carefully at the circumstances in which *The Sign of Four* came to be written. The story was first published in *Lippincott's Magazine* for February 1890, where it is called *The Sign of the Four*, so it would be logical to assume that it was written sometime in the course of 1889. Baring-Gould tells us that Watson married Miss Morstan in May of 1889 and that he 'soon bought a connection in the Paddington district from old Mr. Farquhar'. Watson was therefore setting up a married establishment, building up his newly-acquired practice and attempting to supplement his army pension with a little writing. And, this time, Watson could rely on little help from his friend, adviser and literary agent: Conan Doyle was otherwise engaged. Pierre Nordon in his biography *Conan Doyle* tells us that Watson's colleague's daughter, Mary Luise Conan Doyle, was born 'early in 1889' and that 'in the spring of 1889, April to be exact', Conan Doyle 'rented a hunting-box in the New Forest' where he worked on his great historical novel, *The White Company*.

So, Watson was busy. We may presume that he did a full day on his medical business and worked at his writing in the evening. In fact, we have his word for this. In his chronicle of the 'Boscombe Valley Mystery' (which Baring-Gould dates to early June 1889 – or about a month after Watson's marriage) Watson is unsure as to whether he should answer a call from Holmes because 'I have a fairly long list at present'. It is the new Mrs Watson who says, 'You have been looking a little pale lately. I think that the change would do you good.' Watson would have based his narrative of *The Sign of Four* upon the notes that he kept and the journal that he wrote up 'when the going is slack'. It would have been an easy matter for Holmes to have altered some of the information in the journal and in the notes and jottings. Is it not likely that he altered some of the dates too? How much easier to explain to a recuperating Watson that his brother had died before the occurrence of Watson's enteric fever. Holmes also had an ally he could never have foreseen: Cupid. As any reader of *The Sign of Four* will know, Watson claims to have fallen in love with Miss Morstan almost from the moment that he first saw her. How does this fit in with the fact that he does not mention her in the sections of the present narrative that derive from his pen? I believe that Watson's romance blossomed from the time that Mary Morstan made her 'accidental' visit to Southsea. Holmes, that most efficient of observers, had noticed the way that Watson had been taken by Miss Morstan, and, rightly, supposed that her 'sweet and amiable' expression and her 'large blue . . . singularly spiritual and sympathetic' eyes would be the most effective remedy for the old campaigner. One wonders if Holmes realised, as he encouraged Miss Morstan to make her visit to Southsea, where the sequence of events he was putting in hand was to end. Watson, not yet fully recovered, tired by long hours of work and head over heels in love, swallowed the changes that Holmes had made in his notes without even noticing.

What do we know of Mycroft Holmes's surrogate Watson, Lord John Roxton? We know that he existed since he appears in the book *The Lost World* (Hodder and Stoughton 1912) which was written by the journalist Edward Malone and was edited, coincidentally, by Sir Arthur Conan Doyle! This book tells us that Roxton was 46 in 1912, so he would have been 22 in 1888, which at least does not disagree with the meagre description that Holmes has given us. Nor does the story of Roxton's vendetta with the Shanghai Tong seem out of character. Malone records in his book that Roxton fought a 'little war' on his own against the Peruvian slave-drivers in 1909. 'Declared it myself, waged it myself, ended it myself.' Roxton says that he finished the war by finishing the king of the slavers, Pedro Lopez, 'killed in a backwater of the Putomayo River'. Roxton was apparently so successful in this 'little war' that he was known as 'the flail of the Lord'. There was certainly nothing wrong with Roxton's nerves either. Malone's description of how the explorers gained access to the South American plateau which was their destination shows this. Finding the thousand-foot cliffs unscaleable, they climb a rock pinnacle that is as high as the plateau and situated about forty feet from it. Malone cuts down a tree to form a bridge and the explorers crawl over the precarious bridge trying 'not to look down into the horrible gulf'. All except Roxton that is – 'he walked across – actually walked, without support. He must have nerves of iron.' He had indeed. Incidentally, it is worth noting that Holmes could easily have had the blow-pipe with which he arms Roxton. It would have belonged to Tonga, the Andaman Islander who was manipulated by Jonathan Small and who was killed on the Thames around the 20th or 21st of September 1888. There is no record of Holmes having recovered the blow-pipe but we do know that he had the darts. Watson says in *The Sign of Four* that Holmes 'held up to me . . . a small pocket or pouch woven out of coloured grasses, and with a few tawdry beads strung round it. Inside were half-a-dozen spines of dark wood, sharp at one end and rounded at the other.'

The remainder of the narrative is easily dealt with. For none of it is there any corroborating evidence, but the details may be checked. For example, it is well known that Sherlock Holmes had a brother named Mycroft and that Mycroft was a member of the Diogenes Club; we know from *The Lost World* that Roxton had rooms in the Albany; Holmes was intimately familiar with the opium dens of the East End (in *The Man With the Twisted Lip* Holmes tells Watson that he had found clues in the incoherent ramblings of the smokers and that at least one divan owner had sworn vengeance on him). And the way in which Holmes convinces the policeman that Henry Watson's death was an accident is typical of the way he is able to deduce what had happened from the signs upon the ground, or, at least, to persuade everybody else that he is able to do so.

Now we come to the letters and other correspondence. The memoranda exchanged between the two Holmes brothers make clear how and why the documents comprising the present volume came to be assembled. They also answer a question that has puzzled most of the writers on the Ripper case too: why did Sir Melville Macnaughten, who joined the Metropolitan Police on the 1st of June 1889 (that is, about six months after the last Ripper murder) as Assistant Chief Constable name not one but *three* men who might have been the Ripper in a memorandum that he wrote in February 1894? And where did Macnaughten find these names? In the police files?

No. Those writers who have reviewed the MEPOL files on the Ripper case do not mention the names that Macnaughten does: Mr M. J. Druitt, Kosminski – a Polish Jew – and Michael Ostrog, a Russian doctor. Jones and Lloyd quote Macnaughten's notes in part (in *The Ripper File*) and make the comment: 'This is an extraordinary piece of paper. Macnaughten lists, quite specifically, three suspects whose names are not mentioned anywhere else in any of the Home Office or Yard files. So where did he get them from?' We may suppose that Macnaughten must have obtained the names from Holmes but probably not directly. Macnaughten says in his autobiography – *Days of My Years* – that he spent twelve years in India (though since he says he left for Bombay in October 1873 and returned from India in 1888 it is difficult to see how he achieved this, unless he took long holidays) and upon his return he became a high-ranking police officer. It seems more than likely that Macnaughten would have come into contact with Sherlock Holmes in the course of his work and equally likely that he would also have met Dr Watson. The two men could have found that they had a great deal in common, both having spent time in the sub-continent. It is possible that they might have become more than mere acquaintances and so it is possible – we can say no more than that – that Watson may have told Macnaughten of Holmes's suspicions against the three men named above; particularly after May 1891 when Watson believed that Holmes was dead – killed at the Reichenbach Falls. This is the only reasonable explanation of how Macnaughten was able to pick not one but *three* names out of the air for his memo.

So, wherever it is possible to make a comparison between the incidents recounted in this narrative and what has previously been published concerning either Sherlock Holmes or Jack the Ripper, no significant conflicts are revealed. Perhaps more importantly, the narrative appears to supply answers to questions that have been puzzling people for years. Why was Dr Watson apparently unsure of the location of his wound?

How could Mrs Maxwell have seen Mary Kelly alive six hours after the time of her death? Where did Sir Melville Macnaughten get names of his suspects? – without introducing any new questions of its own.

Sherlock Holmes versus Jack the Ripper: the Obvious Fictions

The idea that the greatest Victorian detective should have tackled the greatest Victorian criminal is an attractive one and so it is not, perhaps, surprising that there have been attempts to produce a story along these lines before now. These previous attempts have largely been obvious fictions, as a brief review of them will demonstrate.

The first version of the story appeared in 1962 in the book that I have taken as my guide to Holmes's life, *Sherlock Holmes of Baker Street, A Life of the World's First Consulting Detective* by W. S. Baring-Gould. The story that Baring-Gould gives is that the Ripper was none other than Inspector Athelney Jones of Scotland Yard. It is certainly true that, according to *The Sherlock Holmes Companion* by Michael and Mollie Hardwick (John Murray, 1962), Athelney Jones appears only in the case of *The Sign of Four* which, as we have seen, is dated by Baring-Gould to September 1888, so he was about in London at the time of the murders and he is not heard of thereafter. Is there any other evidence that he might have been the Ripper? As far as I can discover there is none apart from the fact that he bore a resemblance to the descriptions of the Ripper that we have already looked at. Is there any evidence that he was not the Ripper? I think there is.

Firstly, *The Sign of Four* was published in 1890 and I have suggested above that Watson wrote it during the spring and summer of 1889, that is, after Athelney Jones had been unmasked as the Ripper, by Watson himself, according to the story. This prompts two questions. Would a man with Watson's moral rectitude and his vision of the world in terms of good and evil have written a story in which a sadistic killer was portrayed as a sympathetic character and an efficient police officer, even if that is what he had been prior to his arrest? And, if Watson had chosen to present such a character in such a light, would he not have had something to say of the fact that

Athelney Jones was no longer a policeman, as he surely cannot have been by the time that Watson was writing?

Secondly, there is the way in which Baring-Gould presents the 'facts' of the story in his book. He tells the story and then gives no supporting evidence for it. Indeed, Baring-Gould is careful to point out that the story was given to him by somebody else – a Mr James Montgomery – whose mother, Miss Eliza P. Stephens, was Irene Adler's sister. The story was apparently told to Irene Adler by Holmes himself. As the only evidence that this story is true, Baring-Gould publishes a photograph of 'Sherlock Holmes – From a hitherto unpublished photograph formerly in the possession of the late James Montgomery'. Unfortunately the whole case falls to pieces as soon as it is realised that the photograph is one of William Gillette, the American actor who played Holmes on the stage. According to David Stuart Davies (*Holmes of the Movies*, New English Library, 1976) Gillette played Holmes for 236 performances in New York alone. Any doubt as to the identity of the man is banished when his picture is compared with the one on page 35 of Stuart Davies's book or with that on page 40 of *The Sherlock Holmes Scrapbook* (edited by Peter Haining, New English Library, 1973) both of which show the same man, dressed in the same dressing-gown, and smoking the same pipe, and both of which identify that man as William Gillette.

Baring-Gould also betrays the fact that he has suspicions against Henry Watson by the way he treats him. In the detailed chronology in his book, Baring-Gould gives the dates for the main events in the lives of a number of the major characters referred to in the Holmes saga. The dates of the births of Sherlock Holmes, his two elder brothers, Sherrinford and Mycroft, James Moriarty ('The Napoleon of Crime'), John Watson, Irene Adler and Mary Morstan are all given in some detail (for example, 'Fri., 6 Jan. 1854' for Sherlock Holmes) but no individual entry is given for Henry Watson. The dates of the deaths of all these characters are likewise given (with the exception of Sherrinford Holmes, whose death is not recorded at all) and each is given at the correct point in the chronology. The only major character who does not receive this treatment is Henry Watson. But Baring-Gould does not ignore him altogether. Against the entry recording Dr Watson's birth ('Sat., 7 Aug. 1852') Baring-Gould adds: 'Young John had an elder brother, Henry Watson, Jr., who died of drink in 1888', and this is the only reference in the entire volume to

Appendix

Watson's brother. In dealing with the events of the case of *The Sign of Four* Baring-Gould does not mention the matter of the watch that Watson gave to Holmes to test the latter's deductive reasoning. Why should Baring-Gould be so quiet about Henry Watson unless he suspected that there was more to the elder Watson's death in 1888 than had hitherto been revealed?

The next pairing of Holmes and the Ripper came in the film *A Study in Terror* in 1965. *Kine Weekly* of the 6th of May 1965 states that the film 'is based on an original story by Donald and Derek Ford, scripted by Jim O'Connolly who will also direct' and that 'the picture will have the technical advice of Anna Conan Doyle, the wife of Adrian Conan Doyle, the late author's son'. This technical advice resulted in some remarkable Holmesian reasoning occurring during the course of the film, the best, in my opinion, being that when Holmes receives a case of surgical instruments through the post and is able to deduce that they had been pawned by a medical man who had descended to hard times and that the pawnshop 'faces south in a narrow street, and business is bad. I should also add that the pawnbroker is a foreigner.' Unfortunately, the film's makers did not bother to take any technical advice on the facts of the Ripper case and consequently some elementary mistakes are made. The murder of Mary Kelly (which actually happened on the 9th of November) occurs on the night following the murder of Liz Stride (which actually happened on the 30th September) and no mention at all is made of the murder of Catherine Eddowes who was also killed on the 30th of September. Mary Kelly is shown leaning out of an upstairs window whereas her room was on the ground floor. Holmes askes the doctor, Murray, who has carried out a post-mortem on Liz Stride, his opinion of the knife-work, despite that fact that the Ripper was interrupted in the course of that particular murder and did not have time to mutilate his victim. The Ripper turns out to be Edward, Lord Carfax, younger son of the Duke of Shires, and Holmes is able to work out who one of his victims will be and arrange to be on hand to prevent the murder. Holmes and the Ripper grapple, an overturned lamp starts a fire, the Ripper is trapped, Holmes escapes and Jack the Ripper is reduced to a couple of buckets of ashes. The minor characters are all people of whom nothing else is known: the Duke of Shires, Michael Osbourne, Angela Osbourne, Max Steiner, Dr Murray – none of them is mentioned in any of the published Holmes stories nor are they mentioned in any of the books dealing with the Ripper except that by Donald Rumbelow who briefly outlines the plot and adds the information that the American writer Ellery Queen had expanded the plot in his book *A Study in Terror* which was published by Lodestone in 1966. The story in both cases is an amusing and entertaining fiction – nothing more.

Eight years later Michael Harrison suggested that Watson had let slip a clue that proved that Sherlock Holmes had trapped the Ripper and that the murderer was Mr Harrison's own suspect – J. K. Stephen. Mr Harrison's book (*The World of Sherlock Holmes*) draws our attention to the fact that in the case of 'The Norwood Builder' Holmes makes the following statement to Watson: 'You remember that terrible murderer, Bert Stevens, who wanted us to get him off in '87? Was there ever a more mild-mannered Sunday-school young man?' Mr Harrison considers that Bert Stevens is so close to Jim Stephen that they must be one and the same man. However, Mr Harrison concedes that Watson 'always made some alteration, great or small, in the names of the *dramatis personae*'. Against this I would make two points. If you wanted to refer to somebody called Jim Stephen by another name, would you choose a name so similar to it as Bert Stevens? Neither would I. And the wording of the quote from Holmes (which, incidentally, Mr Harrison does not give in full) strongly suggests to me, firstly, that Bert Stevens was guilty – otherwise Holmes would hardly have called him a murderer – and, secondly, that Holmes did not get him off – Holmes would have said something like 'You remember that unfortunate young man Bert Stevens whom we got off in '87?' if he believed he was innocent and had been able to prove it. It seems to me that what really happened was that Bert Stevens, who really was a terrible murderer, tried to convince Holmes of his innocence and failed. And, if Bert Stevens was found guilty of murder in 1887 I think it extremely unlikely that he would have been able to commit a series of murders in 1888. By that time he would have been hanged.

In 1978 Jonathen Cape published Michael Dibdin's *The Last Sherlock Holmes Story* in which he explains why Sherlock Holmes never caught Jack the Ripper. Sherlock Holmes *was* Jack the Ripper! Or, to make it plainer, Jack the Ripper was Professor Moriarty and Sherlock Holmes was Moriarty. Mr Dibdin has resurrected the theory that Professor Moriarty was merely a figment of Holmes's imagination – possibly due to an over-indulgence in cocaine – based upon his old mathematics tutor. In Mr Dibdin's story Watson discovers Holmes's secret by actually seeing Holmes in the act of mutilating the final victim, Mary Kelly. This would be, of course, early November 1888 and yet Watson takes no action against Holmes until 1891 when he accompanies Holmes on his trip to the Continent which he has described in his story 'The Final Problem'. I do not have to attempt to explain why this story is pure fiction because it has already been done by somebody much better qualified than am I. Trevor H. Hall, author of *Sherlock Holmes: Ten Literary Studies, The Late Mr Sherlock Holmes* and *Sherlock Holmes: The Higher Criticism,* published *Sherlock Holmes and His Creator* in 1978 (Gerald Duckworth and Company Ltd). In a chapter of that book entitled 'Dr. James Moriarty' Mr Hall outlines the career of Holmes's great opponent and in a second chapter deals with the suggestion that had already been put forward that Holmes and Moriarty were one and the same, coming to the conclusion that it is 'unmitigated bleat'. I agree with this description.

The most recent (at the time of writing) attempt to match Holmes and the Ripper has been in the film *Murder by Decree* in 1979. The film's screenplay was written by John Hopkins and the story has been adapted for publication by Robert Weverka. (The copyright of the book is owned by Saucy Jack Inc.) The credits of the film contain the following statement: 'This motion picture is a fictional dramatisation based on recent theories concerning the infamous crimes committed by the alleged "Jack the Ripper" ' and a statement to the effect that the film is based on the book *The Ripper File.* The story line, however, is taken largely from that developed by Stephen Knight in his *Jack the Ripper; The Final Solution.* Knight's theory is that Jack the Ripper was not one man but three: Sir William Gull, physician in ordinary to Queen Victoria; John Netley, a self-employed coach driver; and Sir Robert Anderson, head of the CID – or, possibly, the third man was Walter Sickert, the artist. The film changes the names of the men involved but the story is much the same. In the 1979 revised Star edition of *The Complete Jack the Ripper* Donald Rumbelow discusses Stephen Knight's book and makes the following comment: 'Long before the end of the book, one is asking over and over again "Where's the evidence?" The answer, of course, is that there isn't any.' I support this view. Indeed, I think that the available evidence that we have actually points away from Mr Knight's theory. Mr Knight tells us that John Netley's part in the crime was to lure the victims to the coach, where they were murdered and mutilated by Gull, and then to dump the bodies. This, says Knight, explains why the Ripper was never caught since he did not, in fact, commit his crimes in the street. Unfortunately, the evidence indicates that at least four of the Ripper's victims were killed where they were found.

The first victim, Polly Nicholls, was found in the street by a policeman. All he could say was that there was nobody about at that time and that the body had not been in the street half an hour earlier. It is possible that Nicholls had been dumped from a coach. The second victim, Annie Chapman, was found in the back yard of Number 29 Hanbury Street. The time of the murder was fixed at approximately 5.30 a.m. It is possible that a carpenter, Albert Cadoche, who lived next door at Number 27 actually heard the murder take place. He went into the yard at about 5.20 and heard a voice from the yard of Number 29 say 'No'. Three or four minutes later, that is, within six or seven minutes of the estimated time of the murder, Mr Cadoche heard what he described as a 'sort of fall against the fence'. He did not hear the sound of a coach. In any case, there would be no chance to use a coach since the back yard of Number 29 could only be reached via a narrow passage *through the house itself.* Further evidence that Annie Chapman was killed where she was found comes from the police report quoted by Donald Rumbelow, which, in part, stated that there were 'two flaps of skin from the lower part of the abdomen lying in a large quantity of blood above the left shoulder'. If Annie Chapman had been killed in Netley's coach and her body merely dumped in Hanbury Street the 'large quantity' of blood would not be beside her body: it would be drying inside the coach. The third victim, Liz Stride, was found probably within seconds of her throat being cut; certainly the blood was still flowing from it. Neither Lewis Diemschultz, the man who discovered the body when his pony shied at the smell of blood, nor Edward Spooner, who was standing outside the Beehive public house when the body was discovered and who got to it in time to see that blood was still flowing, mentioned that he had seen a coach. It seems unlikely, therefore, that a coach could have been used in this murder. The fourth victim, Catherine Eddowes, was found at 1.45 a.m. by a constable who had passed that spot at 1.30 and had seen nothing. At

1.35 three Jews saw a man talking to a woman at the entrance to Mitre Square (where the body was found) called Church Passage. Though they could not definitely identify the woman, one of them, Joseph Lawende, thought that he recognised the clothes that the victim was wearing as the same that the woman he had seen was wearing. Neither of these witnesses mention a coach. Nor did the watchman (a Mr Morris) in Kearley & Tonge's warehouse on the north-west side of Mitre Square, even though, according to Donald Rumbelow, 'the door was on the jar' and the watchman came immediately P.C. Watkins called him. Neither the watchman nor P.C. Watkins reported seeing or hearing a coach, so it is extremely unlikely that one could have been used. The final victim, Mary Kelly, was definitely killed in the room in which she was found. Dr Bond says in his post-mortem that 'the blood had flowed down the right side of the woman and spurted on to the wall'. This proves that she was killed where she was found and so no coach was used for her murder either.

Therefore, of the five murders committed by the Ripper four of them were almost certainly performed without the use of a coach and there is no evidence whatsoever that a coach was used in the other. Since the coach features prominently in the killing shown in *Murder by Decree*, the film's accuracy must be regarded as highly suspect. It is not only the details of the murders the film gets wrong either. At one point Watson is shown trying to get some information from a woman in Whitechapel. The woman, taking Watson for a toff out on a spree, and a male accomplice try the old badger game on him. When Watson refuses to be either bullied or blackmailed and calls for the police a crowd gathers. The woman tries to suggest that Watson is the Ripper but is not believed because the crowd think he's too old and one of the policeman who take him away says sneeringly 'he couldn't rip up my old grandmother'. Now if, as Baring-Gould says, Watson was born in 1852, he would have been only 36 in 1888. In another scene, Sir Charles Warren (apoplectically played by Anthony Quayle, who has come up in the world since playing the lowly police surgeon Murray in *A Study in Terror*) throws Holmes out of Mitre Square despite the fact that the square is in the City of London and, consequently, not in Warren's jurisdiction. Such glaring errors must mean that the whole story is fiction and fiction that is none too carefully researched.

So, as we have seen, where the facts contained in this narrative can be checked they are found to agree with the already established facts as published in the books dealing with the Ripper case or the problem of the career of Sherlock Holmes. This, as I have shown, is not true of any other version of the story.